Divine Death

A Jessamy Ward Mystery

Penelope Cress, Steve Higgs

Contents

It started well...

"Careful now, we don't want you falling down the hole, Reverend!"

A voice called to me from the subterranean depths beneath my feet. I edged my way carefully around the timber hoist and red metal safety cordon where only a few days earlier our twelfth-century marble baptismal font had stood.

"Being careful, I promise. How's it going? Any more discoveries?" I called below.

I was curious to know more. The Stourchester Historic and Archaeological Society (S.H.A.S. for short) had been excavating a medieval brick-walled well under the left aisle of St Bridget's for nearly two weeks.

"Better able to explain once I'm above ground," the voice replied.

A tug on the rope signalled that the owner of the voice wished to ascend. On sentry duty above ground stood my churchwarden, Tom Jennings, who jumped into action, cranking the winch handle to bring the 'voice' aloft. The well must have been deep because it took several minutes before a yellow hard hat appeared below the rim. And several minutes more before the wearer of the said yellow hat was safely back on terra firma.

The voice now had a face, and the face, as expected, belonged to Mrs Isadora Threadgill, widow of this parish, chair of S.H.A.S. and a veteran amateur archaeologist. Though

Isadora was about my age, she had the air of a dowager duchess. It was an easy stretch to imagine her holding a torch for Howard Carter in the Valley of the Kings.

Once she had steadied herself and wiped the dust from her horn-rimmed glasses on the bottom of her lilac fleece jacket, Isadora grabbed my hand with all the excitement of a four-year-old visiting Santa's grotto. She led me to a makeshift table in front of the church altar.

"There, Reverend, what do you make of them?"

Presented in a series of white cardboard boxes was a collection of tiny clay figurines.

"Did you bring these out today?" I asked, counting seven boxes on the table.

"Jolly good haul, isn't it? Looks like tributes to some kind of fertility goddess to me. No wonder the Church covered it up all those years, eh? Can't be having all that pagan nonsense in a good old Christian place of worship." Isadora leaned in and breathed the next few words in such a conspiratorial tone, I suspected she was afraid the church walls might be listening. "I think what we have here, Reverend, is arguably one of the most important pre-Christian finds in this area, since well... ever!"

My heart sank a little at her earnest words. A great archaeological find would be wonderful for the island's tourist trade and is certainly of important historical value, but what would that mean in practical terms? It was Pentecost in a few weeks, and I had hoped there wouldn't be an enormous hole in the middle of the church to navigate my way around. Now I had a distinct feeling that the *'we'll be out of there in a few days'* dig was going to go on for some time yet. And more importantly, here was yet another connection to my family's pagan past! A tangible link to the legend of the Wells of the Triple Goddess and all the hocus pocus that entailed.

I took a step closer and picked up one box.

They may have been underground for over two millennia, but these fecund figures clearly had three heads and what I could only describe as outrageously exaggerated child-bearing hips. One didn't need a degree in archaeology to work out that these clay figurines were tributes to a pagan goddess, probably offered with prayers for a successful pregnancy.

"May I?"

Isadora stood legs astride, hands on hips with the proud bearing of a mother whose child had just won a Nobel peace prize, and nodded. I put the box back down on the table, took a deep breath and carefully picked up the offering.

It had a pulse!

I wanted to let go, but the rhythmic current pulsated through my hand and up my right arm. My chest tightened. Everything turned blood red.

"Reverend? Are you okay? I think she's coming round. Quick, Tom. Fetch some water."

My head throbbed. I must have knocked it somehow as I fainted. I reached up to check for blood and realised I still had the figurine in my hand. I fixed my bleary eyes on Isadora and gestured for her to take it back.

"So sorry, I don't know what came over me." My stomach lurched to my throat. "Probably because I haven't had breakfast yet. So embarrassing."

"Nothing of the sort. Happens to the best of us. Let's get you in the choir stall." Isadora fussed.

The welcome sight of Tom's bald head bobbed into view as he returned from the church hall with a glass of iced water. "Barbara's put the kettle on. Some sweet tea and the last of the scouts' Jammie Dodgers should set you right."

I took a sip of water and thanked them both for their attentions, assuring them I was feeling absolutely fine and they should get on with the excavation. I didn't want to hold them up any longer. "I will take that tea next door. Get out of your way."

Despite their protestations, I was keen to get moving. Apart from a sore head, I felt fine. The nausea had passed as quickly as it came. Barbara Graham, my over-efficient parish secretary, would bring tea enough for an army, and if I didn't make a bolt for it immediately, this would slip into a cosy mid-morning tea break that could last an hour or more. I had things to do, places to be - not least on that list I wanted to speak to my aunt

Pamela, or my mother about this little episode before I forgot the details of what I had seen.

Since returning to Wesberrey, I had experienced a couple of similar incidents. It was hard to maintain my belief that they were coincidental when they had helped me piece together clues that had led to uncovering some pretty evil activities. This one, though, was different. No one, to my knowledge, was dead... yet.

But I had seen blood. Lots of blood. And pain. I had felt so much pain. Maybe I should pop into the Cottage Hospital, see my best friend forever, Dr Sam Hawthorne, and unofficially get my bump checked out. Just to be on the safe side. That would be a good reason to leave. Except, I couldn't find a bump. I gently massaged my scalp, but there was nothing. No lump, nothing felt tender to the touch.

The sound of tea things clinking on a tray snapped me out of my cranial examination. I accepted the familiar green cup and nibbled at the jam-filled biscuit. Barbara, sporting new earrings that matched the colourful biscuits on the tray, had loaded the tea with enough sugar to stop my heart in its tracks. I sipped it graciously. Tom had pulled over three chairs to create a circle around me in the stall, and there was no way I could escape. Fortunately, no one felt the need to bombard me with questions, they were just there to offer company, and asking how I was feeling every five minutes was as probing as it got.

The conversation oscillated between concerns about me to curiosity about the figures, via talk about how best to present the finds to the rest of the society, and the world.

"We need to ensure that you get the credit, Isadora," Tom proclaimed adamantly, waving a chocolate digestive in her direction. "I accept you have a lot of respect for DeVere, but I don't trust him as far as I could throw him. Remember when you invited him in to give the society a talk on Roman Britain? All he did all night was sell us his YouTube channel. That man is no better than a snake-oil salesman. He would kill his own mother for a find like this."

Scared? Who? Me?

"**W**ell, there are no signs of concussion. In fact, I can't see any evidence at all that you ever bumped your head. I can send you for an X-ray to make sure."

On arriving at the Cottage Hospital, I had recalled the events of the morning to Sam and despite my protestations that the headache had gone and I was feeling totally fine, she insisted on checking me over. From a thorough head examination, asking me if it hurt a thousand times, to the magic penlight in my eyes to check pupil dilation, my best friend left nothing to chance.

"Sam, there's no need, honestly. I told you, the pain had gone before I finished my first biscuit!"

"Still, with head injuries, you can never be too careful. I would feel better if you allowed me to send you to X-ray." Sam popped the small black penlight into the top breast pocket of her white coat and strode back around to her chair on the other side of the desk. "So, which one of the coven are you going to ask then?"

By 'coven', she meant my mother and her two sisters, Pamela and Cindy.

"I thought I could pop over to Pamela's after I had done my midweek rounds. Which I am already late for." I replied.

"Question, if I may?" Sam was now sitting opposite me. Her hands were busying themselves with a small camel-coloured cloth and the left lens of her glasses. "Why have you been avoiding Cindy?"

"I haven't!"

She was right; I had.

"Jess, you can't lie to me." She was right again. "I have a theory."

"Go on then, Miss 'Ask Me, I'm A Doctor'," I answered in a ridiculously childish sing-song voice that confirmed her suspicions I was on the defensive.

Sam adjusted her freshly cleaned spectacles on the bridge of her nose and leaned in, resting her forearms on the desk to assert that this was a serious conversation.

"You are afraid."

Silence.

She waited.

More silence.

This was intolerable. I finally broke.

"Is that it? Is that your theory? That I am afraid? Well, I don't think Dr Phil has anything to worry about."

"Well, aren't you?"

"No." I squirmed. "Well, not really. I just feel more comfortable talking to my other aunt."

That was true. Pamela was less esoteric, more grounded. Cindy was wonderfully ethereal. Though she had been the first member of my family to tell me the truth about the goddess legacy and the various skeletons in the Bailey/Ward cupboard, I had been avoiding her more of late. In my defence, Mum had opened up more over the past few weeks, filling in the blanks in our family history over the many meat-free dinners we had tested since my youngest sister had decided to open up a vegan cafe in the old bookshop. "And," I added, "Pamela lives closer." This was also true, Cindy lived on the other side of the harbour, past Stone Quay. I hadn't taken my orange scooter, Cilla, back out there since I bought her.

"I think this latest episode needs more personal insight." Sam sat back in her leather chair and folded her arms. "Cindy is the current 'godmother', right? The keeper of the Wells. I am sure the latest finds would fascinate her, and she might shed more light on what you just experienced." She scrutinised my face to confirm her theory, "You *are* afraid, aren't you?"

"No, I am not." But Sam was right. It terrified me. Ever since I returned to Wesberrey at the beginning of the year, I had experienced so many strange things. There was no way I could continue to deny that there wasn't some truth to the family legend. My aunts, my mother, even my sisters all had some mystical gift, some extraordinary ability that I shared, except this power seemed to focus on me. Cindy had predicted that I was the next godmother. The next keeper of the Well of the Triple Goddess. Not that I was sure which well that was. I had assumed it was the one we had gathered around in the bottom of Pamela's garden back in February, but now they had found a second one under the font in the church. And what exactly did I see when I passed out? I've had visions like this before. There was blood. Lots of blood. And lots of blood is never a good thing.

"Look." Sam smiled. "Why don't we go together? I have the afternoon off tomorrow and look at what I bought online. It came yesterday." Sam reached into the bottom drawer on her left and produced a turquoise scooter helmet with navy and white stripes. "It's got a real retro look to it, hasn't it? I thought I would see if Sal has a scooter to match. Then we could go for rides around the island together, now that the weather is better."

"Well, Sal's is on the way to Cindy's and I could do with getting him to check over Cilla. I will call my aunt and check she is free."

"Great, pick me up at one. Now, Reverend, if you are sure you are up to it, we have a few patients who, for some reason, I can't quite understand, would like you to visit them, say some prayers and stuff."

"That's my job. Bringing comfort to the sick and dying." I sprung to my feet. This was my calling, not as some mythical goddess guardian. I couldn't explain these visions, but one thing I knew, there was only one God, and I was already doing his bidding.

Venus de Wesberrey

L ater in the evening at the Parochial Parish Committee meeting, Tom and Barbara were all talk about the morning's finds. They now forgot any concern they had about my little fainting spell amidst the excitement of Sebastian DeVere's scholarly assessment. He believed the figurines were very 'rare examples of stone age fertility offerings' and would greatly interest the British Museum, though he would argue to keep some examples for examination at Stourchester University.

"Mr DeVere was not at all how I expected him to be from your description, Tom. I found him to be the perfect gentleman." Barbara was once again passing around the biscuits, this time a plate of Garibaldis.

Tom threw his hands in the air. "That's how they worm their way in though, isn't it? Charm. Not that I am that easily swayed by a mustard cravat and a well-manicured handshake!" Tom reassured us all. "I can see how his gallant mannerisms and elegant phrases can turn one's thoughts against themselves. He spoke in such glowing terms about our 'Venus de Wesberrey'."

"Venus de Wesberrey? What utter nonsense!" Tom's partner and fellow churchwarden, Ernest scoffed. "Best to wait until Norman has done a thorough assessment before we start naming the finds in such grandiose terms. Venus de Wesberrey, indeed."

"Well, I wouldn't put much stock in anything Norman Cheadle says either." Tom's tone changed, Ernest had obviously hit a nerve somehow. "DeVere may be rapacious, but Norman Cheadle is a vile, ignorant creature. And you know better than to mention that man's name in good company."

Tom flounced away towards the toilet and Ernest bowed apologetically before scuffling after him.

"I'm sorry." I scanned the rest of our group for some explanation. "Who is Norman Cheadle and why does his name upset poor Tom so much? I have never seen them argue before."

Barbara raised her eyebrows at Phil, who sat next to me trying to mind his own business, and with a dart of her eyes sent her fiancée off to check on the warring couple. Phil dutifully made his excuses and followed Tom and Ernest to the lavatory.

"Norman and Ernest. They were colleagues. Years ago. I don't know all the details, but Norman gave up the law to become a historian after he did his PhD at Stourchester. Rumour has it that before he left, he defrauded the firm of several thousands of pounds. Enough to scupper Ernest's pension and retirement plans. He had to use his savings to save the firm. I don't think they could ever prove it was Norman Cheadle. There were no criminal charges brought. But that's why Ernest still worked for Lord Somerstone from time to time. To keep the wolf from the door, so to speak."

Well, that would explain Tom's reaction. Ernest has an incredibly forgiving nature. I admit I would struggle to turn the other cheek in such a situation.

"But why would we involve this Norman Cheadle, given their history? We have Sebastian as our expert."

Barbara puffed herself up and tilted her head towards me. "Norman Cheadle is Sebastian's supervisor, I believe. DeVere would have to confer with him before they go any further. I doubt Isadora is aware of this bad blood. She's not a native islander. Poor Tom."

Poor Tom indeed.

The Experts Have Landed

Isadora had arranged a full appraisal of the Venuses for the following day. To ensure I could get back to St. Bridget's in time for the expected visitation of Norman Cheadle and Sebastian DeVere from the mainland, I made the most of the brighter mornings to get out on my parish rounds as early as possible. It was invigorating to get outside on this crisp spring day. Once naked trees gathered branches of pink and white blossoms close to their chests as I spluttered past, and glimpses of fading bluebell carpets dotted themselves through stone walls and garden fences. Though the air had yet to fully embrace the warmth of the morning sun, it would be a fine Thursday, whatever dramas it held in store.

I was also keen to leave plenty of time to collect Sam for our road trip to the other side of the Island after lunch. I had successfully avoided my mother at the vicarage. She would know something was awry if I saw her. Rosie was the only one up when I finally got home after the meeting last night. She was too wrapped up in the interior design plans for her cafe 'Dungeons and Vegans' to notice me beyond a quick hello as I raided the fridge for any leftovers from dinner. There were calls of 'Get him! What are you doing? Man!' from my study, which meant that Rosie's son Luke was deep in gaming mode. And my eldest sister, Zuzu? I hadn't seen her for days! In fact, we rarely saw her unless 'the Baron' was on an important case or away on business. As I whizzed through the glorious narrow roads of Wesberrey, I thought about how time intensive a new relationship is, and how lucky I was to have time to myself to determine my own schedule. I was so incredibly lucky to be this free.

I pulled up outside a charming, grey-slate cottage on the furthest point east on Upper Road at the junction with Sandy Cove. Wisteria was successfully chasing out the ivy from the sunniest walls of this pretty building, but the ivy remained victorious above the faded green door. So mighty was its grip above the mantle I was wary that rattling the brass knocker too hard would bring down an army of bugs and crawly creatures. Fortunately, the owner of the green door opened it before I found out.

"Reverend Ward, so kind of you to come out so early. I just this minute put the kettle on. Would you like a cuppa? I have some Earl Grey at the back of the cupboard if that's more to your liking?"

"Whatever you normally have will be fine with me, Mrs Jenkins. Now, you had some concerns about the theme for this year's Queen of the May Parade. I understand you usually do the flowers for the float."

So my morning began. Several more stops and many cups of tea later, I was back at St Bridget's just in time to dash to the lavatory before the big event kicked off. As I turned to flush, a vaguely familiar voice called out through the stalls.

"Vicar! Are you decent?"

"Er, yes... almost. Who's there?"

"It's Tilly, Luke's friend."

Tilly? Luke's friend? My nephew Luke. The guy who was never more than a few feet away from a game, either on my ageing computer or his phone, has made a friend? A girlfriend? He never leaves the vicarage! How did that? Oh, wait... Tilly! The exotic dancer from the Aphrodite Club?

I took a beat to settle the shock on my face and opened the toilet door to find a petite brunette who I barely recognised without the animal print mini skirt and tight-fitting blouse. This Tilly was wearing a camel-coloured suede cropped jacket over a pristine, if snug, white t-shirt and baggy blue jeans.

"Tilly! Why, of course. What a pleasant surprise! What are you doing here?"

"Oh, I have been meaning to pop by. My dad bought one of the new builds on School Lane, and I moved in with him a few weeks ago. I wanted to get away from the city. You know what I mean." Tilly lifted herself up to sit on the sink stand and dangled her legs off the edge. Her childish pose made me realise she was barely more than a couple of years older than my nephew, in fact without the heavy make-up she was possibly the same age. How did she end up as a muse at the Aphrodite?

"So, you kept in touch with Luke then, after Lord Somerstone's funeral? I had no idea." I shook the water from my hands and pulled out a fresh paper towel from the dispenser.

"Yeah, we FaceTime regular-like. What's going on in the church? There's a massive hole in the floor of the side aisle!"

"They have been excavating the old well. The Stourchester Historical and Archaeological Society have been here for weeks laying the groundwork, processing the site, and then yesterday they actually went into the shaft and brought up a load of figurines. Fertility offerings, they think. Stone Age. We have an expert coming in a few minutes to appraise the find."

"Ooh, how exciting! I've always been interested in old things. And I'm not talking about the clientele at the Aphrodite." Tilly giggled. "Don't suppose I could tag along?" she asked.

"Ehrm…" I couldn't think of a reason to refuse, well not quickly enough anyway. *What objections could there possibly be to a teenage strip-tease artist joining a meeting to examine mini pagan goddesses found in a well under a font in an Anglican church?* "Be my guest, the more the merrier."

Back at the altar, I introduced Tilly to Isadora. She appeared delighted that someone so young showed interest in her discovery and regaled in telling Tilly all about the various documented stages of the dig. I took advantage of the distraction to check in on Tom, who was looking very sullen by himself on the front pew.

"I think Ernest is very forgiving." I ventured.

"He is a saint." Tom whipped out a polka-dot handkerchief from his blazer pocket and loudly blew his nose with it. "Can you believe he's gone with Phil to greet that charlatan off the ferry? He asked me to join him. I snapped back; why don't you just roll out the red carpet and be done! He looked so upset. I hate us to part on an argument. It's not good for the soul, eh, Vicar?"

"I am sure he appreciates how you want to protect him, but he is being the bigger man here. I admire that." If I were honest, I was more inclined to side with team Tom on this. I may believe in forgiveness, but to act as if it never happened... *Maybe Ernest is in denial?* "Maybe this is his way of accepting the loss. It's only money, after all."

"You are right, Vicar. He has such a strong faith. When I asked him about it last night, he said Norman must have needed it more. Of course he did! He was a mediocre lawyer and is now a second rate academic. I fear he will use this to further his own ambitions. If DeVere doesn't steal his thunder, that is. Poor, sweet Isadora, this is rightfully her treasure chest. Look at her. It is rare to find a woman with such verve, such passion. See how she is talking to that young woman. By the way, Vicar, she looks familiar. What did you say her name was?"

"Tilly. Short for Elizabeth, I think. She, er, her family has recently moved to Wesberrey. One of the new houses in School Lane. Maybe you have seen her around. She is one of Luke's friends."

"Ah, I see. Well, they would make a darling couple."

At that moment the large oak doors under the bell tower swung open, and a series of rapid footsteps scuttled up the centre aisle. I peered over Tom's shoulder to witness a dusty black polyester suit, topped by a shock of white hair, leading the charge towards the altar. An elegant Italian three-piece suit with sandy jaw-length curls strode a few feet behind. Ernest and Phil brought up the rear. I squeezed Tom's hand to offer him a sign of my support and then rose to greet our guests.

"Gentlemen, welcome! You must be Dr Cheadle." I outstretched my hand to the black suit, who grunted acknowledgement and clumped straight past me. Instead, the slim fingers of Mr Sebastian DeVere met my hanging palm.

"Reverend Ward, such an honour to meet you at last. Please excuse the professor, he's a man of few words." Or manners, I thought to myself. "Sebastian DeVere, at your service. Please, shall we join them at the front? It really is quite the find, you know."

After much peering and pursing of narrow lips, Dr Cheadle eventually turned to Phil and said, "Mr Vickers, do you still own the Cat and Fiddle on Market Square?" A surprised Phil nodded in the affirmative. "Splendid, well, two rooms. One for myself and one for young DeVere here. We shall be back in the morning to take over. No one. And I mean *no one* is to touch anything without my say so. Is everyone clear? DeVere? We shall return to Stourchester to fetch our things. Reverend." He nodded. "Mrs Thurgood? It's been a pleasure."

Before anyone could correct his error on Isadora's name, Norman Cheadle pivoted on his heels and marched back out of the church with equal urgency to that of his arrival. Sebastian bowed and followed behind him.

The rest of our party stood looking at each other open-mouthed.

A nasal trumpet brought us back with a jolt.

We all turned to Tom, who was casually folding his handkerchief back into his pocket.

"I'm warning you. Nothing good will come out of having any dealings with that man. Mark my words."

Travellers' Bay

I knew Mum would be down at the bookshop/cafe with Rosie and Luke, so I snuck back to the vicarage to grab something to eat before setting off again to see Aunt Cindy.

I had thought a lot about Sam's words. Maybe I was afraid. Cindy was the current keeper of the Wells of the Triple Goddess. Her prediction was that I would succeed her and then, in my turn, pass the honour down to one of my nieces. I was still struggling to accept this. I was, after all, an ordained priest in the Church of England and until only a few months ago had considered women such as my aunt as misguided hippies and, at worst, witches. Now I was having visions and experiences that I couldn't argue away with Anglican doctrine. I have always been very liberal in my approach to faith and have tried to embrace all cultures and beliefs. I believe there is one true God but, as Jesus said, there were many rooms in his Father's house. I believe in the power of prayer. I know God in my heart. None of these recent happenings had dimmed the light of His love inside me. My faith had grown stronger. But I feared having to give up the priesthood. How could I be a pagan goddess protector and be a shepherd to my flock?

I took a few moments to gather my thoughts and sent a little prayer for clarity to the Boss Man. If there was one thing my faith had taught me, it was to let go and let God.

*****

16

Minutes later I was heading west to Sal's Scooters with my best friend riding pillion. The day was living up to its morning promise. Flecks of afternoon sun danced through the fresh green canopy along the roadside down to Market Square. The sea joined them in a dazzling light show as we turned onto the harbour front. Wesberrey could hold its own against the delights of the Amalfi Coast today. In fact, one could have been mistaken for thinking we had slipped through a portal into an Italian postcard as we rounded the final bend to be greeted by a rainbow of gleaming Vespas and Lambrettas.

I took advantage of Sam's detailed inspection of the scooters to check the map before setting back off for Cindy's house. I was ashamed that in the four months I had been on the island, I had never ventured out this way. Most of my parishioners lived on the east end of Wesberrey or close to its commercial heart. Cindy had always met me in town or visited me at the vicarage or at Aunt Pamela's, and before I bought Cilla, I had no easy way to get out to this side of the island.

The western cape was historically an outpost for 'vagrants and minstrels', which would explain the appeal to my aunt. Cindy was a free spirit with timeless grace and beauty. She seemed to glide effortlessly through life, depositing love and wisdom in the hearts of all who met her. How on earth was her plump, frumpy niece supposed to take over this crown? But, despite my sister, Zuzu, being a better candidate on paper (she looked the part and certainly believed in free love) both of my siblings were mothers and the godmother is childless. I guess that was my only qualification.

Once Sam had settled on a brand new sky blue Vespa Primavera model to match her new helmet and handed over a huge wad of cash to pay for it, we began the gentle climb around the cliff head to Travellers Bay. The main coastal path ran all around Wesberrey and linked all the island's major arteries. As there were no cars, there was also no need for most of the roads to be much more than a dirt trail, the only traffic being the occasional horse and cart. Even so, it was important not to get lost. We needed to find the correct turning, or we were likely to trespass onto private property or, even worse, territory owned by the Royal Navy.

As children, we were always warned away from visiting this side of the island because of the real danger of being shot at. The navy had evacuated the base after the Falklands War, but I wasn't keen to find out if they still had any security on-site, especially those guards with waggy tails and sharp teeth. Fortunately, Sam spotted a scrappy piece of plywood with a faded painted arrow on the roadside. We took the next left.

The tarmac road soon dissolved into loose gravel and clay, making the last few miles of the journey a true test of our scooters' suspensions. We carefully followed the line of telegraph poles that ran alongside the path as the road vanished beneath us. The flat landscape flanked us for miles on either side. As we alighted our mechanical steeds at the entrance to the picturesque hamlet, my inner thighs and rear end screamed their gratitude. We continued into the wild west of Wesberrey on foot.

Travellers' Bay had a peculiarly desolate charm. Pastel cottages nestled amidst the sandy dunes. It was like standing in the middle of a dusty watercolour painting. Nothing had any real definition, there were no edges, no boundaries. One of these shapes was my aunt's home, but which one? There were no street signs or house numbers, just names: 'Higgins', 'Bartholomew', 'Simmons' and 'Bailey'.

"Here we are!" I triumphantly announced. I stopped by a pale lilac timber clad building with an array of pampas and other ornamental grasses acting as a garden. Sam took off her helmet and adjusted her glasses. Typically, her sleek bun had remained perfectly coiffed, no sign of being flattened. I didn't need a mirror to know that my cheeks were ruddy and my hair was more tangled than Christmas lights straight out of storage.

"Welcome, Jess, darling!" Cindy air-kissed me on each cheek. "And Dr Sam! How marvellous. I wondered how long it would take you to pop along to see me. I'm afraid I only have herbal tea in at the moment. I'm on a bit of a detox to prepare for Beltane. Though no chamomile, I'm afraid. Can't stand the stuff, tastes like grass. I can offer you dandelion root or peppermint. There might be some Rooibos somewhere?"

Sam and I both agreed that dandelion root sounded intriguing.

I'm not sure what I expected from Cindy's home. I knew it wouldn't be the floral and beige mood board of Pamela's house, but I guess I expected it to be more extreme, more gothic, more witchy? The room I sipped tea in was a sumptuous bohemian lounge with a tasteful vibe in muted pastels. There were lots of plants hanging in macramé holders from the ceiling and shelves. Delicate shawls layered the dusty pink sofa I was sinking into. More shawls draped over the stunning white peacock wicker chair Sam perched upon. Cindy held court from a sage brocade chaise lounge in front of a trio of pine bookcases, each shelf stuffed full of paperbacks and curios. The other walls hung with original artwork. Some pictures were of my aunt in her youth, several were nudes.

"So, darling child, you had another blackout."

How did she know that? I hadn't mentioned a word to anyone except Sam. I cast an accusatory glance in her direction.

"Don't look at me! I didn't tell her!" Sam huffed.

My aunt gracefully kicked her legs up onto the chaise to prepare for what she obviously thought was going to be a long conversation.

"Jess, why does this continue to surprise you so? They found the well, didn't they? Was it under the font? We had often suspected it was there. It would have to be on the convent side of the church."

"The convent side?"

"Yes, to the left of the stone arches. There were two chapels before the Reformation. Two altars. One for the nuns, the other for the community. They sectioned it off by a curtain to offer the nuns some privacy. That half is the only surviving part of the abbey. The rest was torn down during the dissolution of the monasteries. It only survived because of that shared wall. The curtains are gone now, of course. You must have realised there's an extra aisle?"

"Yes, no one ever sits there as you can't see the altar." I was possibly more shocked that my aunt knew so much about the architectural history of the church than I was that she knew about my fainting spell.

"Exactly. It was always a small house. Never over thirty sisters. The only other surviving part of the convent is the stone archway that now leads into the hall. You must have noticed the Green Man carved into the frame?" I shook my head. Green men often appear in older churches. Probably a nod to the pagan sites they stood on, or the continuing rural traditions of the local stonemasons at the time. "It's no coincidence you have discovered those simple offerings so close to Beltane. Or as you would call it, May Day. The Green Man is preparing to emerge from winter's restorative temperance. He will soon walk abroad, infusing all living things with his passionate fire."

Sam giggled. When Cindy turned her way, Sam recoiled sheepishly into the wicker chair like a naughty schoolgirl. "Sorry," she added, "It just sounded like he is feeling a little horny."

"Oh, he is. He's a great lover. He sows his seed across the land, and Mother Earth is aching to receive him. You can feel the anticipation in the air. The yearning of the trees, their blossoms heaving with desire."

I coughed. "Well, I had never thought of May Day quite that way before."

"Really?" Cindy smiled. "All those virginal young things dancing around the maypole. All seems pretty phallic to me. Would you like another cup? No? Right, well let's get back to your vision then. Was there a lot of blood?"

Tilly

I returned home to find the kitchen table covered in fabric swatches and pictures of hipster eateries. Mum and Rosie were comparing wallpaper designs. At the far end, Luke was sharing headphones with an unusually coy Tilly. Their fidgety moves clear signs of the attraction they both felt for each other. It was almost primal. Musky. Intoxicating. Teenagers! Ugh! I needed coffee.

I kissed Mum and Rosie on their cheeks and made my apologies, citing paperwork and the need to take advantage of Luke being distracted to get onto my computer. Tilly was making herself at home. She seemed a lovely young woman, but I admit her past troubled me. It didn't seem of concern to the rest of my family, and certainly not to Luke. I was probably being overprotective. And I was probably reading too much into their body language. All that talk of seed sowing and heaving bosoms from Cindy had corrupted me.

Anyway, his mother and grandmother are a couple of feet away. What harm was there in being hospitable to a new neighbour? I fired up the computer and set to work through my To-Do pile. As usual, Barbara had efficiently labelled my correspondence with handy Post-It notes so I could clear through everything in about half an hour, giving me plenty of time to look into the provable things my aunt talked about, namely the history of St. Bridget's and the nuns who used to live here.

I was deep into a website on the Rules of St. Benedict when there was a gentle knock on the door.

"Reverend Ward, may I come in?"

The door cracked open a few inches and a pair of eager eyes peeked through the gap.

"Of course, Tilly. How can I help?"

Tilly wandered around my office studying the various books on display with far more interest than I had ever shown them. They came with the vicarage and looked impressive, but I had no idea what hidden gems filled the shelves.

"I love old books, don't you? Do you mind?" Without waiting for my answer, she pulled out a dusty green hardback and scanned the index. "Perhaps S.H.A.S. would be interested in this one. It's the history of the parish by one of your predecessors." She flipped back to the title page. "A Reverend Algernon Fortescue. Sounds cute."

"Anything, in particular, I can help you with? I'm rather busy." The harshness in my voice as I spoke surprised me. I wasn't at all busy. Maybe I was just tired.

"Oh, yes, sorry Reverend. It's just... I wanted to talk to you. About my past." She walked over to the fireplace and paced back and forth, adding physical momentum to the words she had to get out. "I want to make a clean start and, well, I know the last time you saw me my tits were hanging out of a cotton tunic, but I am out of that game now. Honest. I am thinking of going back to college. Maybe to study literature or something. I love to read. I... well, my mother, she's an addict. Any money went on her habit, not the rent... anyway, someone had to pay the bills." She stopped pacing and looked at me, directly. "I never slept with the punters, you know. Nothing like that. I mean, if those sad bastards want to pay to see me dance around in my nightie... what's the harm, eh? It's their money."

Tilly was clearly an admirably resilient young woman. "I'm sorry you had to work in a place like that."

"Well, no one would work there if they didn't need to, would they?"

"No, I suppose not." I was angry at myself for my naïve comments. "Do you mind me asking, how old you were?"

"Fifteen, I think. Not Stavros's fault, I told him I was older. I mean, he might have guessed, he never asked for my birth certificate or anything."

"Stavros, he's the club's owner, right?"

"Yeah, he's actually a proper gent. Looks after his girls. Paid us well, made sure we all got home safe and stuff."

I imagined he was more concerned with protecting his assets than their safety, but who am I to judge, except that is exactly what I had been doing. *He who is without sin.* "What made you leave?"

"Dad came to one of my shows! Can you believe it? I haven't seen him since I was a baby. He rocked up with some business clients and well... I recognised him straight away. Mum kept a photo of them both taken at the funfair on the mantel. I'd studied that photo so closely, I knew every laughter line. He looked just the same."

Tilly had settled herself down with Fortescue's history on the chair by the fire. I felt the need to join her. It was obvious she wanted to talk, and I would do a better job of listening away from my desk.

"So, what did you do? Did he recognise you?" I asked.

"I carried on dancing. One thing you learn really quickly in that game is that no one is looking at your face. Anyway, the last time he saw me I was still in nappies. My arse has changed a lot since then!" Tilly closed the book and fixed me with an anxious stare. "I'm sorry. You must think me really... What's the word? Uncouth. No, vulgar. Talking of tits and arses. I forget I'm with a priest sometimes. I don't mean to offend."

"No offence taken, I assure you. Please continue."

"Well, when the number was over, I explained to Stavros why I couldn't go back out there. He was furious at first. I was his... let's say my 'dance of the seven veils' had quite the following. There would be some seriously pissed, I mean, angry, punters. He threatened to not pay me. The rent was due. I mean, I was desperate, so we struck a deal. I would earn my keep that evening waitressing and he wouldn't give me the sack. But I owed him one. Still do. I quit the next day."

"So how did you end up living here with your father then?"

"I served his table. Waitresses are even more invisible than dancers. I told him we had a problem with his credit card and the payment may have gone through twice. I asked him to leave his details behind so we could contact him if there was a need to refund him. Total nonsense, of course, but he was too drunk to process what I was asking him for."

I shuddered to think how the men in these clubs behaved after a few drinks and what these poor girls had to deal with. "I hope your father did nothing inappropriate?" I blurted out and immediately chastised myself for vocalising such a disgusting idea.

Fortunately, Tilly appeared to find the idea very amusing. "No, thank God! He was adorable. His business partners were a little frisky. Those chiffon tunics don't offer much protection, but nothing I couldn't handle. Anyway, I got what I wanted and went around to see him the following day."

Tilly pulled her denim-wrapped legs under her and rested the closed book on her lap. For a moment she seemed to drift away, then with a sigh, she added, "I have never been so scared in my entire life. I mean, nothing gets to me, you know? But it was like I was returning home the conquering hero after an epic adventure. I was saying to Luke the other day..."

"You told Luke all this?" It surprised me, their friendship was obviously stronger than I realised.

"Of course! I tell him everything. He's such a brilliant listener. Most guys aren't interested in what I have to say. Anyway, it's like you've been on this quest, searching for the magic key that will unlock your heart's desire and then it's like there, within your grasp and it could all turn to dust."

"But you have a happy ending?" I offered.

"Yes, the happiest. Dad has been wonderful. He asked me to live with him and helped find Mum somewhere to get help. She's where all those celebrities go to dry out. And I get hot showers every day and the chance to get to know him." I wanted to enquire more about the showers but checked myself. Clearly, someone struggling to meet the rent might also have issues with paying for boiler repairs or even gas or electric. "I mean, Reverend, he ain't no saint, and he still buggered off and left us when I was a child, but I'll take this over my old life any day. Which brings me to why I wanted to talk to you."

I had forgotten Tilly had started this conversation. What could she want from me? "Go on, if there is anything I can do to help, just ask."

"I want to be the Queen of the May!"

Through Fresh Eyes

F riday morning began, as usual, with my weekly visit to the primary school to join their assembly. Every Friday passed much the same. The school secretary, Audrey, was thawing to me gradually, but I knew we would never be best friends. I was getting to know the other teachers but looked forward most to my weekly chats with the head teacher, Lawrence Pixley, who was in an ebullient mood.

"Fantastic news, Jess, the school is getting a makeover!" The school was very shabby and a lot of general maintenance was long overdue. If duct tape ever becomes a design trend, Cliffview Primary would be a show home. "It seems we are a beneficiary in Lord Somerstone's will. Such generosity!" Lawrence clapped his hands excitedly. "Lady Arabella visited yesterday, there's just one small caveat."

I eyed Lawrence sceptically. My experience with the late Geoffrey Somerstone made me nervous to ask what conditions he had placed on this bequest. Lawrence's raised eyebrows suggested he wanted me to ask, so I swallowed hard and ventured, "What, Lawrence? I can't even begin to guess at the inner workings of that man's mind."

"We have to rename the school." Lawrence stretched his lanky frame to its most commanding to deliver the next line, "You are looking at the principal of the Somerstone Academy for Education and the Arts."

"Impressive. I am delighted. So how much money are we talking? Enough to give the reception area a lick of paint, I hope."

Lawrence bent back down and took hold of my shoulders. It was impossible for him to contain his excitement. "Jess, there are millions of pounds in trust. Arabella will become our patron and I want you to sit on the board. We are going to create a forward-thinking, technologically enhanced centre for the creative development of young minds. I can hire new teachers, build new classrooms. There will be a garden, vegetable plots, a zip-wire!"

"A zip-wire?"

"Yes, from the mound at the back of the playground. The kids will love it. And we will open the new resources to the community. That's why I need you to work with me on this."

I had never really noticed what handsome eyes Lawrence had before. Admittedly, I had never noticed his face full stop. It was a kind face, with features as gentle as he was, but his constant sniffing had always distracted me. I was also acutely aware of his habit of pushing his glasses back up his nose as a punctuation mark at the end of each sentence... *That's what's missing! Is he wearing contacts?* I tried to look, without looking, to see if I could see that tell-tale circular rim around his irises. I couldn't see a lens, but they were an interesting agate green. This was now feeling a tad awkward. Lawrence still had my shoulders in his grasp. I felt the need to say something, anything to ease the tension.

"Love you. Love to. I mean, I would love to work with you on this. Sorry, just got carried away with..." *Jess, don't say your eyes whatever you say, don't say your eyes.* "Your ey-excitement!" *Nice catch!*

"Wonderful, I was thinking, if you have time, of course, we could discuss the plans. Maybe over dinner? Er, tonight? I hear that the Old School House has a Spring Lamb special, a two for one offer. Not that I wouldn't spring for the full price, sorry awful pun."

"Tonight? Can I get back to you? The family has some Beltane thing planned...."

"I understand." He shrunk back like a deflated Air Dancer outside a car showroom.

"No, I want to. Honestly, I've never eaten at the Old School House and… I just need to check, okay? After this, I will pop home and ask Mum. I'm sure they can go ahead without me."

My cheeks burned throughout the school assembly. I was very aware of Lawrence standing beside me. There was a buzz, a frisson. Even the children singing 'All things bright and beautiful' couldn't dampen this fresh energy. Their normal cacophony appeared temporarily replaced by a heavenly choir. God's light filtered through the skylights, washing the hall with an amber glow. The squeaky melodicas were in harmony with their angelic little voices, and miraculously in time with their headmaster's accordion. The recorders were still a little pitchy, but the overall effect was delightful.

I skipped back to the vicarage. When I say 'skipped' I mean I trotted more lightly than usual. I cut through the graveyard. Tilly was helping Luke feed the local wild cats. I had never seen him smile so freely. I waved at them as I passed, but didn't stop to chat. I was sure they preferred to be alone, and I wanted to catch my mother before she set off. She was so busy lately, helping Rosie to get everything organised for the new cafe.

"You look nice this morning, dear. Is that a new blusher? A bit of make-up makes all the difference. You should wear it more often." Balanced on the second to last step on the stairs, Mum was dangling a cat toy of silver bells and coloured feathers into the hall. Hugo, the family's adopted ball of claws and sinus threatening dander, was in full primal hunting mode, determined to catch his bouncy prey.

"Mum, I'm not wearing any make-up. I must be just a little flushed from the walk back from the school. By the way, glad I caught you. When I was around Cindy's yesterday, she mentioned that it's Beltane and I wanted to check if you had anything witchy planned because I might need to excuse myself. I have a prior engagement." *That's only an acceptable little white lie, right? I am sure the Boss has bigger concerns right now.*

"Yes, I thought we could all run naked through the graveyard. Pamela's been cutting back on the carbs in preparation." She laughed. "Why…" Mum abandoned the game and moved in closer, her eyes interrogating my face and smiled, "Have you got a date?"

How does she do that?

"I have a business meeting with Lawrence Pixley to discuss plans for the school. Seems we aren't the only ones remembered in Geoffrey Somerstone's will."

"Hmm." As usual, Mum's mood soured at the mention of *that* name. "Is there anything His Lordship doesn't have his tentacles in? Well, I suppose at least this is to do some good."

My mother was still struggling with the long shadow Lord Somerstone's involvement with our family continued to cast. I hugged her. Unusually, she seemed happy to receive it. As I pulled away, I cupped her face in my hands.

"And his legacy is going to do us good too," I said. "It's giving Rosie a fresh start and I am sure we can put my share to good works in the community."

"I know. It's okay, dear. I'm getting used to the idea. Funny old world, eh? So you and the headmaster. He seems like a good man. Tall. Blond. Musical. There's a bit of the Peter O'Toole about him, I suppose."

"Yes, seems his mother was a fan, hence his name. After Lawrence of -"

"Arabia!"

"Exactly. And it's not a date, Mum. Just business. There's a two for one offer at the Old School House."

"Of course, just business, I understand," Mum smirked at her reflection in the hall stand mirror. "Don't you worry about Beltane, dear. Sounds like you're heeding the call of the Green Man in another way."

Quote, Unquote

C alling Lawrence back to accept his dinner invitation threw my stomach into more knots than a tub of two-day-old cockles from the stall on Harbour Quay. In fact, I had barely eaten anything all day and had only had one cup of coffee so far. Maybe it was tea and biscuit withdrawal. Usually, by this time of day, my stomach would be swimming in digestives and PG tips. Never fear, there was bound to be a kettle on in the hall where I was eager to catch up with Professor Cheadle and Dr DeVere.

Opening the heavy main doors was likely to disturb the group's concentration. I wanted to take some time to observe proceedings before shattering their deliberations with the sound of slamming oak and iron, so I entered through the side door as quietly as possible. If people knew that the lock on the door was so rusty that we never secured it anymore, the altar candlesticks would be on eBay before we could say 'holy communion'. Therefore, it was a secret entrance privy to only a trusted few. It took several weeks before Phil took me into his confidence, and it's my church!

There was a knack to opening it quietly, though. The trick was to push with just enough force to budge the door from its ancient frame anchor without setting the heavy cast iron handle a knocking. In the winter, when the wood freezes, that's almost impossible, but I hoped that the warm sun had warmed it up just enough to enter as quietly as the proverbial church mouse. I felt like a criminal, but it worked. Soon I was lurking in the curtains of the Lady Chapel. The acoustics were perfect, and I was safely out of sight.

Tom had set up the trestle table from the Hall in front of the altar and they had added more boxes. I tried to count them, but Sebastian DeVere was partly obstructing my view. He had a clipboard in his hand and was diligently taking notes as Norman Cheadle paced up and down the altar, gesticulating as if he was the keynote speaker at a political rally. Isadora was sitting with Tom in the front pew, hanging on Norman's every word.

"The overarching question remains. Do these figures qualify as Venuses? In 'Celtic Civilisation and its heritage'. Cite Filip. Note Sebastian to check the year of publication. Where was I? Ah yes, In Filip's seminal tome he reminded us that Macrobius, quote 'Holds this squatting position to be characteristic of deities of fertility and fecundity.' Unquote. Hence the lack of arms. They are intentionally part of the moulded sculpture in a form people of the time would have easily recognised as being that of a woman in labour. There can be no dispute, therefore, that like the famous Venus de Willendorf, these incredible finds are indeed Venuses."

As Norman finished, Isadora rose to her feet and applauded loudly. Sebastian slung his clipboard under his arm and joined in. Tom's response was rather more subdued. He was the first to speak.

"Great, well. I suggest we break for lunch. I'm amazed you have any voice left." Tom dramatically checked his watch. "My, just over an hour. DeVere, you poor boy, your wrist must be fit to falling off! I will get the sandwiches out of the fridge. I am sure Barbara has put together a charming spread." And with a flick of his hand to gesture that they should all follow him through to the hall, Tom marched away.

The rest of the group followed in due course, with Cheadle leading from the front. "After lunch, Sebastian, we will settle on a date, but I suspect those objects predate the Christian site by several millennia. That bronze form you found this morning though doesn't tie in with the rest. I suppose it could be a later interpretation of the goddess. The markings appear Celtic but the metal used refers to a much earlier period. I believe I have seen something similar before. When do you say they built the convent?"

Sebastian pulled the clipboard out and flipped back a few papers. "670 A.D."

"Yes, typical time period for the establishment of Anglo-Saxon churches in the county..." His voice trailed off. Sandwiches sounded good. My stomach was rumbling. But first I wanted to get a quick peek at the latest finds.

There were now ten boxes, all with similar rounded figures, some clay, some wax, but one was clearly different. It was the same basic shape as the others, but more ornate with swirls carved into its metallic brown body. I wanted to inspect it, but after what happened last time, I decided it would be better to wait until there was someone with me.

My stomach grumbled its agreement with me. Food first. Figurines later. I wondered if Barbara had also made some cake.

Dinner for Two

L ate in the afternoon, I had one final check-in with Barbara before I could get myself ready for my business meeting with Lawrence. I had heard so much about the cuisine at the Old School House, but their prices were well beyond that of a parish priest, and I would have thought that of a headmaster as well. The only other option, until Rosie opened Dungeons and Vegans, was the Cat and Fiddle. *And* the very real issue of having our conversation interrupted by the landlord, Phil (my verger) or his fiancée, Barbara (my secretary) or any number of other locals (most of them my parishioners and/or the parents of Lawrence's pupils). Though it was a simple business meeting, two attractive, single pillars of the community such as us, dining alone together, would set tongues wagging.

And he *was* attractive and single and a pillar of the community. *Jess, stop yourself! It's business, just business. And yesterday you didn't even consider him as date material. You didn't even consider him at all!* But what to wear?

Trust Barbara to have some views on the subject. "I hear Pixley has finally summoned up the courage to ask you out." I knew there was no point in asking how she knew. I imagined that the whole island knew by now, and there was I naively worrying about the gossip mill after the dinner! Barbara sighed, "He's just like my Phil that way. Very shy. Only took him fifteen years to pop the question."

"It's not a date, we are meeting to discuss the new academy."

"Of course, of course. You could do a lot worse than Lawrence Pixley, you know. I think green. Red is too obvious. Blue will wash out your complexion, you need warmer tones. Shame you don't have time to get your roots fixed at 'Scissor Sisters', that bob they gave you last time was the bomb!"

"The bomb? Barbara, have you been at the communion wine?" I laughed. "I will find something suitable, I promise. But first tomorrow's parade. I spoke to Mrs Jenkins and sorted out her concern about the colour theme, so that's all good to go."

"And my Phil has repainted the maypole. It's looking splendid. He is so talented."

It was so endearing to hear Barbara talk about her Phil. After all those years too afraid to admit their feelings for each other, things had moved on a pace since their engagement at Easter. They had set a wedding date for June, and it promised to be the highlight of the year.

"Now, I know that the Queen of the May crown is highly prized and usually a competitive process, but erm, in the event of a tie who gets to make the casting vote?"

"Why, you, of course, Vicar." Barbara was busy stacking flower garlands and plumping out the paper petals. "I think we've been using these same headdresses since I was a girl."

"They're very sweet. And who handles the count?"

"Well, over the past few years we have left that responsibility to Ernest. Everyone else is too busy setting up the pole in the square and putting the finishing touches to the float. Except back in 2006, when the horses pulling the float bolted. All hands to the chase on that one. The poor queen and her attendants were almost at the far side of the island before one of the fairies, or whatever they were, straddled the lead horse and brought it to a halt!"

"That sounds terrifying! And the vote, I guess that's open to all?"

"Of course. We used the tombola. Everyone puts their vote in the hatch. Then during the dance, Ernest counts the results. Why, Reverend Ward, you look concerned. It's not Miss World, just a bit of harmless fun!"

"Yes, yes, of course. It's Tilly, remember her? Well, she is entering and asked me to help her win. Well, she didn't actually ask me, but she wants to win so badly."

"Oh, I know who you mean. I've seen her downtown with young Luke. She's a beautiful girl. I daresay she will win in her own right."

"I agree, Barbara. I daresay she will."

*****

Nothing is worse than waiting for your business partner to join you at a meeting. He was only ten minutes late, and I was early. I wasn't sure how to act. Do I order a drink whilst I'm waiting? *A glass of water is acceptable, right?* I wish I had brought a book. I could get out my phone, but that might look like I'm bored, or impatient, or even rude? What did I ever do on previous dates?

It's not a date!

We said at seven o'clock, right?

Fifteen minutes. I'm not counting. *Very probably held up by an anxious parent.* He lives with his mother, maybe she's sick. He would call and let me know if he wasn't coming.

Jess, get a grip!

The Old School House interior was not as I expected. I assumed the decor would match the French cuisine, flamboyant but classy. Instead, they used the old school furniture that was left behind when the new Cliffview Primary opened. They had uncreatively draped old mismatched wooden tables in crisp white linen. There was a nod to romance in the candlelit balloon vases that acted as centrepieces, and the off-white bare plaster walls gave it a slightly rustic feel, but the overall effect was underwhelming. The wooden chairs were uncomfortable, my rear was already going numb, and it had only been... I pulled up my sleeve to reveal my watch, twenty minutes.

Ten tedious minutes later, Lawrence appeared at the door, his head bowing slightly to clear the frame. All thoughts of discomfort ebbed away. He had a certain boyish charm. I had never dated a blond man before. *Jess, this is a business meeting, remember?*

After a few minutes of earnest apologies about being late, Lawrence relaxed and asked for the wine list. And as business meetings go, there was nothing of any note to report. Just a schoolteacher and a vicar sharing some Moules Marinière and a bottle of Chenin Blanc over an impassioned conversation about the local school's future. Absolutely nothing newsworthy in the mirrored body language, how we raised our glasses at the same time, or both went for the last breadstick together. The shared gasps of pleasure as we tasted the tender meat of the spring lamb special offered no greater insights than that the vegan menu would fully satisfy neither one of us at my sister's cafe when it opened. But the acid test of our potential business partnership was still to come. The dessert trolley. Would he pick wisely?

"I think I will go for the Tarte Tatin, with cream. Jess, what would you like?"

Bingo!

"That sounds perfect! I'll have the same."

*****

Lawrence insisted on walking me home. I hadn't plucked up the courage to ask him about his glasses all evening, so embolden by the Irish coffee we had had at the end of the meal, I stopped dead in my tracks and popped the question.

"Lawrence, I have been meaning to ask, and apologies if this seems presumptuous, but are you wearing contact lenses?"

"Ah, not quite, I had Lasik surgery a week ago. So that's why you were gazing into my eyes all evening. And there I was, hoping you fancied me!"

Jess, don't blow it!

I shivered.

"Here, you're cold. Take my jacket." Lawrence took off his blazer and wrapped it around my shoulders.

"But, I do fancy you," I mumbled as I turned to face him. This was a risk, but it was Beltane after all. *The Green Man is stoking the fire, all I have to do is light the match.* At that moment, the moon slid out from behind the clouds and bathed us in silver.

"Jess, may I?"

I nodded. He leaned down. *I may need to wear heels again.* His lips brushed mine, gently at first. Soft, hesitant, then more confident. *Oh my!*

"Do you end all your business meetings this way?" I joked "I'm not sure Audrey would approve."

"Well, my meetings with Audrey don't end like this, that's for sure!"

"I'm relieved to hear that."

We linked arms and strolled down the final hundred yards to the vicarage. My sisters would have plenty to say about this recent development, and as for Sam, she had always ribbed me for my taste in pretty boys with cow eyes. Lawrence was not my usual type, but perhaps that was a good thing. He was younger than me, but what does that matter in this modern world? He must know I am too old for children. No need to have that difficult conversation, surely? *Jess, stop that right now! It was one kiss!*

I was happy though. Like songbirds had nested in my heart.

We stopped outside the vicarage, both of us suddenly more bashful than we had been only a few minutes earlier. *Oh no! He is having second thoughts! Told you not to get carried away...*

Lawrence bent down and planted another tender but deliberate kiss on my lips.

"Guess I will see you at the May Day Parade tomorrow then, Reverend Ward."

"I guess so, Mr Pixley. Thank you for your coat." I reluctantly removed his jacket and handed it back, not wanting this moment to end.

Lawrence's eyes held mine as he backed away the first few steps back before turning to go. There was a smile. I was sure there was a smile. *Look back.* He cast a quick glance over his shoulder.

He looked back!

I fumbled for my keys in my bag. My heart pounding so loud in my chest, I thought it would raise the house. I shouldn't have worried, Mum was still up. She opened the door just as I reached for the lock.

"Jess, come inside, dear. Dave's on his way."

Dave? I was confused. Why would the unsociably late arrival of my sister's boyfriend concern me?

"Oh, I had a great evening, by the way. If you're interested, he kissed me. And it was lovely. No tickly moustache, either. I may just be a *little* bit drunk. If you don't mind Mummy dearest, I will retire before our honoured guests arrive."

"You haven't heard?"

"Heard what?" I stumbled over the threshold into the hall.

"It's Norman Cheadle. Jess, he's dead. Luke found his body in the church!"

Blood, Blood and More Blood

There is nothing like the news of a sudden death to sober you up. Whatever was waiting for me at the church, it was time to throw on the clerical collar and don the blackest of outfits. My sister Rosie had already gone to wait with Luke. He had called the vicarage, then Mum had notified the police. The local representative of which, PC Taylor, was taking down Luke's statement when I arrived.

"So, can you explain to me again what you were doing in the church, after dark?"

"I told you already! Wait, do you think I did it?" Luke had obviously been crying. "I saw the light was on and I heard a noise. Mum, I wasn't... I didn't, I mean..." Rosie put her right arm around her son and used her free left hand to put a cautionary finger on his lips.

"He will not say another word until he has a lawyer."

PC Taylor rolled his eyes, tutted, and made a display of flipping his notebook shut and slipping it back into his breast pocket. "So be it. I suggest you return to the vicarage then. I am sure Inspector Lovington will have more questions for you. Ah, Reverend Ward. I was wondering how long it would take you to appear. I hear the lamb special is delicious!"

Everyone knows!

"I came as soon as I heard. This is my church, Constable. Have you examined the body? Are you sure he's... dead? Luke can have quite the imagination."

PC Taylor stepped aside to show me where Norman Cheadle lay. There was so much blood. I felt faint.

"Oh, he's dead as a doornail, Reverend. As to the cause of his untimely demise, I should say the heavily blood-stained candlestick is a likely murder weapon, wouldn't you?"

I could barely bring myself to look. I had never seen such a horrific sight. Whoever had taken Norman Cheadle's life today wanted to make doubly sure he wasn't coming back.

"Have you called Dr Hawthorne? You will need an official pronouncement of death."

"The county coroner is on their way. And, before you ask, Reverend Ward, I have already called Bob McGuire, and the ferry is heading to the mainland to collect the Inspector as we speak." I detected a hint of passive-aggressiveness in PC Taylor's voice.

"I'm sorry, I know you have everything under control."

"I have. I am a trained police officer and this is not my first murder investigation. Until he arrives, Inspector Lovington has put me in charge. It is my responsibility to secure the crime scene. So if *Master* Luke has nothing more to say..." He coughed. "I want you all to go back to the vicarage and wait. And no one is allowed to leave the island."

Rosie helped her son to his feet. He was visibly shaken by the evening's events. I had plenty of questions for Luke, but as we headed home, he had one for us.

"Did that copper just make a Star Wars reference?"

Yes, Master Luke, I believe he did.

*****

Knowing that nothing hits the spot like freshly baked food and a warm cuppa after a shock, Mum had thrown together a simple spread. A delicious Victoria sponge, some sandwiches and a fresh pot of tea stewing under the cosy sat on the kitchen table. Luke was ravenous and dived straight in. Rosie, understandably, was feeling a little queasy. She was, though, the first to talk.

"Mummy, it was horrible, horrible. My poor baby, stumbling upon that horrid scene! Luke? What were you thinking of going into the church? What if they had killed you too? Did you see them? Oh my God, did they see you? Will they come and hunt you down whilst you're asleep in your bed? Will they kill us all?"

"Sis, please calm down. I think whoever killed Norman acted in the spur of the moment. They took whatever was handy. It was a murder of opportunity. I doubt they will want to add to their crime. Wherever they are, they are probably very frightened, right now."

"Of course, I forgot, you are an expert in murderer's motivations, silly me thinking you did a degree in theology, not criminal psychology!"

"Rosie, dear, Jessamy is only trying to help."

It was never a good sign when Mum used my full name.

"And I am sure that she too will keep away from getting any of us any more involved in this affair than we already are."

"But, Mum, PC Taylor thinks Luke's involved somehow. I can't let my nephew -" Mum cut me short.

"And neither will Dave. What is the point in having one of you sleeping with a police inspector if we can't use that to divert attention away from our family?"

"Grandma!" Luke kicked back his chair. "You think I had something to do with this!" He harrumphed. "I didn't. I found him, that's all."

"But it looks bad. You understand you will be a suspect. Look at you, you're covered in blood."

"I had to check for a pulse. I tried to do the mirror test with my phone, which was stupid, I know, and then used the torch to look into his eyes."

"And all that blood wasn't a big enough clue? Luke, I despair!" Rosie reached out for a sandwich and shoved it into her mouth as if doing so would gag her thoughts.

She choked. A little. Nothing life-threatening, but Mum showed ninja-like stealth in her response, hitting her firmly between her shoulder blades several times before the rest of us had even processed the situation.

Luke's blue eyes were widening in frustration.

"Mum, I did the right thing. He was dead, and I called you straight away."

Rosie took a beat to force down the remains of the sandwich. "Yes, and *they* are going to twist that. Why didn't you call the police straight away, eh? Did you think we could come and clear up the crime scene?"

Luke glared back at his mother. His manic black curls shook around his head in defiance. "I didn't do it!"

"Of course, you didn't." I looked to Rosie, her son needed her unquestioning support.

"Man! This family! Aunt Jess, you believe me?"

I nodded, but I agreed with my sister. This didn't look good. Inspector Dave Lovington, aka the Baron, was an excellent investigator, I tried to assure everyone that he would work it out.

"Jess, dear, your blackout. You saw blood, right? Did you see who killed him? You must've seen it."

"Mum! How? Oh, Cindy, of course. I didn't really see anything, just blood."

Rosie wailed. "There was so much blood! How can one man have so much blood in him?"

She was getting more hysterical with every passing moment. It scared her, naturally. She was normally so calm, so collected. She was the one we all relied upon in a crisis. But since her separation, she was different. More fragile. Luke was her world after Teddy did the dirty and she lost the business along with the life she had worked so hard to build. Mother and son had bonded over the new cafe, forging a different life together, and now this! I worried that this would be the proverbial final straw.

"I think everyone is in shock. Rosie, you know Luke had nothing to do with this, and Luke, you know we believe you. Everyone is just upset and understandably frightened. It's not nice to think that man died in my church!"

"Someone murdered him!" Rosie screamed.

The time for tea and sympathy had passed, and what we all needed now was something a little stronger.

"I think some whiskey would help settle our nerves. I will make us all a hot toddy. That's medicinal, right?" Mum offered. "Luke, you had better clean up."

"No Mum, I think he should wait until Dave gets here. He may wash away vital evidence."

"Yes, Jess, you are right. Still, we can have a nightcap?" We all nodded. Luke looked up from beneath his dark fringe. My mother smiled, rubbing his curly mop. "Even you, dear. After all, you are over eighteen and you just had the biggest shock of all."

The hot toddies warmed and comforted us all. Though they were more honey than whiskey, they were very efficacious. It's at times like this one realises how fragile life is. I had shared similar sandwiches with Norman Cheadle earlier that day, and now he was dead. I believed Luke didn't kill the eminent professor, but felt that there was something he wasn't telling me. I suspected the reason was something to do with Tilly, but I kept that thought to myself, for now. Everyone was upset enough already.

It took another hour and a half before Zuzu finally burst through the door with the news that the Baron had gone straight to the scene of the crime and would follow her up shortly. The waiting was the hardest bit. Norman Cheadle's blood was drying on Luke's skin and clothes. This must be so hard for him. But the worst part was knowing that the real killer was out there with plenty of time to clean up and remove all evidence of their involvement.

I wished my premonition had been more useful. I was in no doubt that what I had seen had been Norman's death, but what use is such foresight if I couldn't warn him or be able to use it to identify his killer? *What a worthless gift.*

"Well, I say, whilst we are waiting." Zuzu pulled over a kitchen chair and nuzzled up to me like an over-keen puppy. "We'll all take stock and interrogate my little sister about her big date!"

"It wasn't a date!" I blushed. "It was a -"

"*Business* meeting," they sang in unison.

Laughter is the greatest medicine, though I suspect the whiskey helped too. And whilst the tension had lifted, I was uncomfortable sharing the more intimate details of my evening in the wake of discovering a dead body in the apse. I hoped for more 'business meetings' with Lawrence and until then wanted to hold the sensation of his sweet kiss in my heart as a refuge from the craziness that was sure to unfold over the coming days.

"We had a very pleasant evening, thank you. The food was lovely, though overpriced if you ask me. I honestly think the Cat and Fiddle is better value."

"But not as romantic, eh?" nudged Zuzu. She caught my simpering expression and knew there were more juicy details to extract. "You don't have to tell us if you don't want to, spoilsport, but I smell *l'amour.*"

"Oh, they kissed. Jess told me when she got in earlier." Mum beamed. "You thought I wasn't listening, right?"

"Where are the bloody police?" Luke put his wrists together, mimicking being in hand-cuffs, "I'll hand myself in. It's better than having to sit here and listen to this soppy nonsense!"

May Day, May Day!

T he 'bloody police' were trampling in and out of my church. The late-night ferry had brought a full forensic team to support Inspector Lovington's investigation. In the wee hours of the morning, Dave had finally taken Luke's statement and collected his clothing in clear bags, suitably labelled. These plastic bags now sat in cardboard boxes on an evidence table hastily set up in the church. The SOCO team had been working throughout the night and were now taking a quick break. I used the pretext of pouring out the second round of tea to sneak back into the crime scene.

The front pews, to the left of the altar close to the excavation of the well, were cordoned off with blue and white police tape, as was the left aisle and apse. A white tarpaulin sheet covered Norman Cheadle's body. A small group of investigators gathered at the rear of the church. In their white scene suits and overshoes, it was impossible to tell if they were male or female, fat or thin until I was very close. As they were resting, they had all either pushed their masks down below their chins or on top of their heads; it was all that differentiated them. It was a surreal sight to watch their blue gloved hands passing around plates of egg and cress sandwiches. These were obviously the least popular filling, as all the other plates were empty.

"Anyone for a refill?" I asked. Several cups sprang out, and I dutifully filled each one. "How much longer do you think you're going to be?"

"That all depends on when the coroner gets here." A familiar voice answered from behind me. It was Inspector Lovington. The white suits all stood up to attention. "Ten more minutes, guys, then back to work. Hope you don't mind if I take the vicar away for a few questions?"

Dave took my elbow and guided me back down the centre aisle.

"I was only playing Mum!" I protested.

"I haven't accused you of anything yet, which now makes me very suspicious that you were up to no good. This was a very violent attack, Jess. I need you to promise me you will leave the detective work to the professionals this time."

"I wanted to get a handle on how long they'd be. We have the May Day Parade at noon."

"And that starts at the school, right? You can lead them along Back Lane to Wesberrey Road and down to Market Square that way. No need to come anywhere near St. Bridget's. I need to minimise traffic in the area. You understand that, don't you?"

"Yes, just one question."

"I ask the questions." He had that cheeky twinkle in his eye. The one that used to make my knees turn to jelly. I want to say it held no power over me anymore, but that would be a lie. It was, however, significantly weakened. He was my sister's beau, and my knees had another cause to tremble.

"Yes, of course. I just wanted to check that you had dismissed Luke as a suspect. Rosie is freaking out and the poor kid has been through a lot lately." We stopped at the front of the centre aisle at the edge of the police cordon. My eyes darted over to Norman's body.

"Jess, you can't get involved in police business. I will do what I can for Luke, but I can't protect him if he's involved."

From nowhere, my heart quickened suddenly, and the muscles in my face and shoulders tightened. I leant in, grabbed Dave by the arm, and growled, "You want to be family. I know you do. Family protects. I know you can protect people when it suits you. So make this suit you, *Baron*."

Where did that come from?

My legs buckled.

"Jess! Jess! Are you okay?"

A white blur of SOCOs moved towards me. *My head, what was that? So sharp!* My vision dimmed. Marble, plaster, and ancient wood spun around me. *I'm going to be sick!* I grabbed Dave's arm.

*****

I woke up propped up on cushions on the sofa in the morning room of the vicarage.

"The May Day parade! What time is it?"

I tried to sit up, but Mum firmly pushed me back down.

"Dear, you have to rest. Everyone is in town and..." She glanced at the clock on the wall behind me as she readjusted my blanket. "I imagine they are dancing around the maypole right now."

"Mum, I need to be there! I'm the master of ceremonies. Why am I here?" I must have passed out again, and for much longer than before. My mind was blank. At least there were no rivers of blood this time - at least not that I could remember. I lifted a hand to examine my head for the second time in four days.

"Dave and some of his fellow officers carried you back. He called Cindy first, asked if you needed to go to the hospital, but she said you would be fine. She's in town but will be here later. Right now you need to rest."

Nothing Mum said made any sense. The situation was beyond confusing, but I didn't want to rest. I was wide awake. Full of energy, in fact.

"I don't understand. Why call Cindy? Why not you? Or Sam? Seriously, I could have needed medical assistance." I pushed myself up. I wanted to get up, but Mum was sitting on the edge of the couch. I couldn't move unless she got up. I tried making puppy-dog eyes to win her round. "Please, Mum. I need to... go to the loo."

She hesitated.

"Mum, I promise I'm not going anywhere. I just have to go... you know."

"I will get you something to eat." Mum bent over and gave me a kiss on the forehead. Then she rose and walked, deep in thought, towards the French doors overlooking the garden.

Mum had taken over the care of neglected flower beds through the early spring and her hard work was bearing fruit. "The Goddess will protect you," she mused, "She is working through you now. I can't imagine what you are experiencing. Only Cindy has that level of knowledge. I thought taking you away was the right thing to do. But, there is no avoiding your destiny." She hugged herself as if hit by a sudden icy blast of air.

"Mum, why didn't Dave call Sam? Why back here and not the hospital? Wasn't he worried?"

I stood beside her, to join in her surveillance of the garden. She kept her arms wrapped around herself and stared ahead.

"Cindy asked him to keep a watch over you. She saw, she -"

"She knew I was going to faint? Mum! Don't be ridiculous. Are you telling me she had a premonition of me having a premonition or some such nonsense? And she didn't tell me but told a police inspector?"

"Yes, I guess. She called me too, to prepare. She will be here soon. She will explain everything to you then." A deep breath followed. "Right, that tea isn't going to brew itself. I thought you needed the toilet?"

When she finally turned to me, I could see tears clinging to her lower lashes. Her furrowed brow at odds with the smile she forced from her lips. I knew there was to be no more discussion. There were no words. Just tea. Just cake. Just comfort. It was all she could offer.

The silence continued over lunch.

My mother was a practical person. A doer. She fixed things. She wasn't a dreamer; she said little, but when she spoke she commanded your attention. She had great love in her heart. So much love for the three of us. It was easy to forget that she virtually raised us on her own. We felt no loss. She sacrificed for our happiness on a daily basis. A trait my sisters and I had shamelessly taken for granted. She was slow to anger, resistant to hate, but when you hurt her, she carried the pain with her always. This pain would manifest in the odd barbed comment, but mostly it caused her to turn in more on herself. Her silent thoughts ruminating on how she couldn't 'fix' this, whatever *this* was. I wanted to hold her and tell her everything would be okay, but Mum would push away any offer of comfort. She always did. That rebuff in its turn added to the many layers of guilt she was already feeling. It was best to accept the tea and stay quiet, for now.

The many questions whizzing around my head were only going to be answered when everyone returned from the May Day festivities. The clock ticked by and gave me plenty of time with my own thoughts. What had happened to me? What had I experienced? Was it connected to the murder of Norman Cheadle? And if so, why? Was it because it happened in my church? Was that my connection, or was that the connection to this goddess thing I couldn't explain or truly understand? I had to assume that Norman was murdered over the discovery in the well. Were the figures cursed? That was a crazy thought. I don't believe in curses. It was far more likely he was killed at the hand of someone who wanted either to stop him doing or saying something.

What are the main motives for murder? Money, love, revenge? Or ambition? Cheadle was clearly excited by the find, as was his assistant Sebastian DeVere. Isadora Threadgill had made the discovery. Perhaps she felt Norman was going to take all the credit. And my own sweet Tom hadn't been shy in stating his dislike of the man and his hatred of what he had done to Ernest.

I couldn't think about Tom being so violent, but who knows what any of us are capable of when provoked. Tom loved Ernest very much. Or maybe it was Ernest, himself. Perhaps turning the other cheek proved just too hard and when the opportunity presented itself... wham!

But none of these theories explained what Norman was doing in St. Bridget's late at night. There was no way that Phil would have allowed them to stay behind after his usual rounds to secure the building. Unless it was Phil? Though why would Phil kill Norman Cheadle? I couldn't think of any motive.

There was the side door. Perhaps it wasn't as big a secret as we thought. Maybe Norman and an accomplice snuck back in after Phil locked up and his accomplice hit him over the head. But why?

Was anything taken? I had no answers. My dramatic fainting spell made sure of that. I knew nothing. Unless my aunt was going to explain who killed Norman Cheadle later, I was going to have to find out myself.

The Queen of the May

The sun was snuggling up under the cloudy duvet of the night sky when Cindy and the others returned from the town centre. I had slipped off to my study. As Mum wasn't in a mood to give me any answers, I might find some elsewhere. Cindy found me curled up in the armchair with a copy of Fortescue's island history.

"Ah, there you are, darling! Good to see you looking so well. I imagine you have a lot of questions for me." *There was hardly anything particularly psychic about that insight!* I needed to check my attitude if I was going to find out the truth.

As I had had many hours to ponder what was happening, I knew exactly what my first question was going to be.

Cindy made herself comfortable in the matching chair by the unlit fire and waited. She oozed with a serenity and wisdom that can only come from the complete confidence of knowing. Knowing what was right, knowing your place in the world... I used to have that, well I thought I did. It's why I became a vicar.

"Well, fire away!" Her silky clear complexion reflected the dusky hues of the evening light of the rising moon. The moon was her satellite. Was I really supposed to take over from her? Cindy's spirit animal was clearly a snowy owl or an arctic fox. Mine was more likely to be a chinchilla or a wombat.

"You're right, I have a thousand questions and we will get to them, don't worry. All I ask is for no more of these mystical half-truths and riddles. Whatever is happening to me is happening fast, and I'm scared. So, do you promise to be honest and open, not to hold anything back anymore?"

"I do."

"Okay, well my first question is, just before I passed out, I wasn't very nice to Dave. I spoke to him with hate. My words were spiteful. They came from somewhere, or should I say *someone* else. Why?"

"Because it was someone else."

I sat waiting for more, but that was it. I could feel my ire rising again.

"Aunt, you promised no more riddles! Who was it?"

"I imagine it was the late Professor Cheadle. The recently murdered do tend to have a bit of an attitude problem I find." She beamed in response.

"So, you are trying to tell me I was, what? Channelling his spirit somehow, and he was using me and my thoughts to have a dig at the police inspector?"

"Something like that. What exactly did you say?"

"You mean you didn't see that in your premonition? And why not warn me? Eh?"

"Because one has to be extremely careful not to change the future. Would you, perhaps, have avoided the church if you knew?"

I thought carefully before I answered. The honest response was that I couldn't know. I wanted to go to the parade. I wanted to see the dancing and the floats, and I wanted to be there to see Tilly crowned Queen of the May.

"Was she?" I asked.

"Darling, was who what?"

"Tilly, was she made Queen of the May?"

"Of course she was. She's exquisite. She reminds me of myself when I was younger. It is so wonderful to witness a young lady so confident in her charms. Luke is smitten, and rightly so."

"Where is she now?" I wanted to congratulate her.

"Oh, celebrating with the other young people, as is right and fitting. This is their time."

"And Luke?"

"Is with her, of course. He is very protective. Good to see there is so little of his father in him." Cindy ran a hand through her silvery hair and smiled. "Now, I am sure you have many more questions."

"Was it Norman's death I saw before? When we talked the other day, you said it could have been any number of things, that blood doesn't have to mean death, but it did. What is the point of these visions if I can't understand them? And, are you saying I can't or shouldn't warn people?"

"Did you know who to warn? No. Jess, your powers are growing. To intervene would be to interfere with that process. I sympathise, it's hard to understand, but I had to stand back. I could sense that something bad was coming and I could connect it to the excavation. I saw you faint into the inspector's arms, but I knew no more than that. So, I asked Dave to call me when it happened. Which he did. In the past, you have seen shadows or heard disassociated voices. Sometimes we have only breadcrumbs. They can help us, but you will never have a complete picture."

"And that's the other thing. Why does the Baron do your bidding so unquestioningly? I get you helped him to understand his wife's suicide, but it's all a bit convenient, isn't it? And him and Zuzu, you thought he would be attracted to me! You were wrong!"

Cindy reached out from her chair and rested her hand on my knee. "I can't tell you any more about Dave's wife. It's not my place. He thought me a total loon when we first met. People are very sceptical, and your bunch are largely to blame for that."

"My bunch?"

"The Church! This isn't a war, you know. We are all accessing the divine. But your Church has preached that those of us who have, say, more of a direct line, are in league with the devil. We are not. You are proof of that. You're a good Christian woman and here you are channelling angry dead men. There is no devil. Only good and evil. Good happens when we are closer to the divine. God works through us. Evil happens when we turn away."

"Okay, well, I'm almost with you there. The devil is the temptation to act against God, to choose our own wishes over his. But surely the smashing of someone over the head with an altar candlestick is the work of the devil?"

"I think you will find it is, as it always is, the work of someone very much of this realm." Cindy slid back into her chair. "I wish I could give you clearer answers, but the way to enlightenment is through opening up your heart and your mind. When you have been willing, the divine has worked through you. To help us connect, we all have our traditions. We have Beltane and Imbolc and, well, you have Easter and in a few weeks, Whitsun. I can train you to handle this better, to read the signs, but you need to find your own anchors. You will become more open to these messages. Sometimes they will terrify you, other times you will feel actual pain. But, there is no need to give up your faith. To find peace, however, you will have to embrace your destiny."

A Girls' Night In

Dinner that evening started as an all female affair. Luke was presumably still celebrating with Tilly, and Dave was busy with the business of detecting. Aunt Pamela had joined us, as Byron had a model railway enthusiast gathering in the Midlands, somewhere near Coventry.

"He has been talking about this convention for weeks, I'll be glad when it's over."

"Well, then Aunt Pammy, what do you suggest we do tonight as we are man-free for the evening? I am up for cracking open the sherry and watching some Magic Mike." Zuzu needed to stay occupied to mitigate her boredom at being Dave-less for an evening.

Rosie was less keen. "Don't you think Channing Tatum has tiny ears? Don't see the appeal, myself."

"Aw, Rosie, you're so sweet. I doubt anyone else was looking at his ears!" Zuzu sniggered. "But I'm sure we can find something on Netflix. Or a board game? Cluedo! Jessie that would be right up your street."

Pam approved. "Did you know they call it Clue in the States? Crazy, eh? And they based Monopoly on an educational tool to teach children about the problems with capitalism."

"Pam, darling, I think you have been spending way too much time locked up in that house of yours with just Byron for company." Cindy joked.

Pamela's mouth twisted, her nostrils widened to suck in the surrounding air. "You are always poking fun at my husband, but he's a good man. Stable. Reliable,"

"And boring! Come on, Pam, darling. Let your hair down."

"Cindy, why do you always do this? Beverley, defend me here."

My mother's habit of silence safely removed her from their argument. For my sisters and I, it was quite amusing to watch their sibling rivalry play out. The three of them were so different. I guess Zuzu, Rosie and I have very contrasting personalities too. That's just the way with sisters, even those with 'special' gifts from the goddess. Eventually, their disagreement petered out, and the conversation moved onto general chit-chat.

"I thought our Queen of the May was stunning today," Pamela said as her eyes scanned the table for leftover hummus to dip her carrot stick into. "Jess, she was all talk about you and how supportive you've been since she arrived."

"Tilly, yes. I'm so sorry I missed it. You know I think she and Luke are seeing each other."

Rosie was quick to defend her son. "Jess, I think your imagination is putting two and two together and making five! They're just good friends."

Zuzu shrieked with laughter so loud she sent Hugo scurrying out into the hallway. The poor cat had been gently falling asleep in her arms. "Luke's not a child! Trust me, they aren't playing monopoly tonight."

"Susannah!" Mum's displeasure was clear from her use of Zuzu's proper name. "Poor Hugo!" She pushed away from the table in search of the terrified pet. "I suggest we move to the other room and find a nice film."

Not that my mother was a prude, she just avoided all confrontation wherever possible. No one likes to think of their children in that way, much the same way as children can't think of their parents having sex either. The fact was though, if not tonight, then surely it was only a matter of time before Tilly and Luke took their relationship to the next level. They were constantly in each other's pockets. Which begged the question, where was Tilly last night? Why was Luke on his own when he discovered Norman's body?

I offered to clear up the dishes and asked Rosie to hang behind to help. The others could pick the entertainment, we would be along later. I wanted to know if Luke had mentioned anything else about last night to his mother.

"I tried to get him to open up," Rosie said. "But he was so upset. I'm worried this will become some deep-seated trauma, you know, buried away in his psyche, only to come out years later on a psychiatrist's couch when he's on his third marriage."

"Did he say any more about what he was doing there?"

"No, he just won't talk to me. He gets all defensive. He thinks I'm accusing him of doing something wrong. Maybe Zuzu is right. Tilly is a dangerous influence. She seemed such a polite young lady."

"In Zuzu's, and Tilly's defence, she didn't say that. She just hinted, very heavily, that they would be getting to know each other more, er, intimately. And, much as that is a difficult thought to process, she's probably right."

"But she was one of those dancers, wasn't she? Those clubs are full of wise guys."

"Rosie! Seriously, wise guys? She wasn't working at the Bada-bing on the Sopranos. It was a gentleman's club. A little seedy, I grant you, but from what she told me, she only danced and did a bit of waitressing. She has a fresh start here; besides Luke is a good boy. I am sure he will do the right thing."

"Yes, like his father. Men, they're all the same." She sobbed. "I don't want my little boy to…"

"Grow up?" I took my detergent-soaked hands out of the sink and carefully put my arms around my baby sister to hug her, without drowning her in soapsuds. "He will always be your little boy. You don't need to worry, you did a good job. He's a credit to you."

"He's still a man, though, and men are stupid! If that Tilly girl is involved in any of this, he is naïve enough to cover for her."

Whilst I couldn't agree with the generalisation that all men are the same or are stupid, it was hard to ignore that love, especially young love, could make fools of us all.

I squeezed my sister as hard as I could. I resolved to talk to my love-struck nephew as soon as possible. I couldn't think of any reason Tilly would have to kill Professor Cheadle, a man she only briefly saw the day before. But perhaps they had a shared past; maybe from the Aphrodite. Such thoughts could wait. The opening bars of 'Be my baby' by the Ronettes were creeping down the hall which meant only one thing: we had agreed on an evening of 'Dirty Dancing'!

The White House

The SOCO team were still finishing up in the church, so we held Sunday mass in the hall. As it was a fabulously sunny morning, I didn't expect the higher than usual numbers, but I suppose a murder brings out the curious. Phil and Barbara had carefully arranged the seating and refreshment tables between them. Rosemary, as usual, was in charge of the hymns, though without the organ had to turn to a more modern form of accompaniment. I went over to help her with the speaker.

"I can't work out this confounded contraption. Phil gave me his smartphone thingy and said I only had to press play but..."

"Have you turned on the Bluetooth connection?" I offered.

"The what?" Rosemary was all confusion. I gestured to her to hand me the phone. I pressed the screen twice to access the correct area and music waltzed into the hall.

"Oh my, that is clever! Your ancestors would have been burnt at the stake for that a few centuries ago." Rosemary took back the phone, let out a tremendous sigh of relief, and sat back in her chair. "So I just hit these double line things when it's over?"

"Yes, I believe it queues all the hymns up in order. Quite the crowd, eh? Though I think they are all a little disappointed we aren't in the church. Even without a dead body, it's too dangerous with that enormous hole." I flopped down beside her. "Rosemary, do you ever wish you hadn't agreed to something? This whole thing is quite crazy."

"Well, that poor man's death aside, the discoveries are important, and if this crowd is anything to go by, will bring more tourists here this summer. I think you made the right decision. This mess will soon clear itself up. It always does, doesn't it?"

"Yes, I guess it does. Right, I need to grab my sermon notes and check on how Mr Pixley is doing with the choir. They looked quite squashed in that corner. Are you sure you're okay here?"

Rosemary smiled. "Don't you fret none about me, you get over there to young Lawrence, clickety-split."

Old age brings an enviable serenity. Though Rosemary could get flustered with new technology and often other people, underlying these bouts of anxiety lay a sense of peace and certainty one can only secure with passing time. Strangely, whilst I viewed Rosemary as an old woman, my mother was probably a similar age. Both were still active and spritely, yet it hit me how much we were asking of my mother to sell her house and move back to Wesberrey, after all these years. Were my sisters and I being selfish to expect her to give up the life she had made, the things she had gathered around her like a comfort blanket, to keep house for us? I had assumed her reluctance was because of all the terrible memories she had here, but perhaps she feared starting over. This was a huge ask, and I hadn't given it any thought. I may be a good shepherd, but I am a terrible daughter!

*****

I am also a pretty awful vicar, as it wasn't until we mingled for tea and biscuits after mass that I realised that neither Tom nor Ernest were there. Though I desperately wanted to hang around more with Lawrence (we hadn't spoken since Friday night) there was a more pressing need to tend to my flock.

After a few gentle enquiries, I learnt that Barbara had been in touch with Tom first thing, and apparently both of my churchwardens were suffering from some undiagnosed malady.

"They said not to worry, just a few sniffles. I don't think they felt up to facing everyone, to be honest. The whole island knows about Ernest's former business partner and well, wagging tongues can be very sharp."

It was time to visit the White House.

*****

I went back to the vicarage to grab some baked goodies, courtesy of my sister's cafe experiments, and like an older version of Red Riding Hood, skipped along with my basket to visit Tom and Ernest. My logic was that they would be unable to resist the aroma of vegan carrot cakes smothered in faux cream cheese and pistachios. It smelt divine.

Tom opened the door. It was well into the afternoon and yet he was still wearing his pyjamas, even if they were topped with a very dashing paisley housecoat. "Ernest has a cold, Reverend, and I'm not too great myself. Thank you for popping by, though, it's very kind."

I wedged my foot in the closing door. "Tom, I understand that you don't want to talk to people, but I'm not people, am I? I am your friend. Please, I promise not to stay long. I just want to see if I can offer you both some comfort at this difficult time."

Tom glanced briefly into the house, and then slowly backed away, letting me enter. "I'll put the kettle on. Those squares look intriguing."

"Vegan," I added as I slipped through the doorway. "We have lots more if you like them. Rosie is becoming a baking whizz. One thing about my little sister, she throws herself one hundred percent into anything she does."

Though Tom and Ernest lived so close, or perhaps exactly because they lived nearby, I hadn't been inside the White House before. I usually saw them in and around St. Bridget's or when they operated the funicular railway. As the tourist season had begun, the railway could afford to pay some local youngsters to staff the two stations, giving Tom and Ernest a bit of respite from their active volunteering.

Their house was much as I expected it to be, a stylish, modern yet classic interpretation of a Victorian home. They had painted all the walls white or in contrasting tones of grey, with odd black feature walls for dramatic effect. Eclectic wooden furniture jostled for prominence against luxurious soft furnishings. The lounge boasted a sumptuous blue velvet sofa flanked at either side by soft brown leather armchairs. Every piece bore the patina of being much loved and well used across the generations.

Ernest had his back to me when I arrived. Huddled over some papers at a walnut writing bureau. On both sides, bookcases filled with dusty hardback covers in various hues lined the wall of the alcove. I coughed to get his attention.

Ernest stuffed the papers into a buff folder and closed the bureau. "Reverend! How lovely of you to honour our little home with a visit. Please sit down. I trust Tom is seeing to some refreshments."

"Yes, he is, and I brought some cakes. Vegan, I'm afraid, but they are lovely." I made myself comfortable on the velvet sofa, it was so lush I couldn't help running my palm up and down the armrest a few times in admiration.

"Vegan? Ah yes, Rosie's plans for a cafe. I am hoping to hand over the keys soon. Lord Somerstone's estate is quite complex, as you can imagine. I hear you have agreed to sit on the new Academy's committee, excellent news. There is quite a lot of money in the trust for that. Lord Somerstone has been incredibly generous."

"I believe he has. Mr Pixley is extremely excited about the possibilities." I tried my best not to kick off my shoes and sink back into the comfy cushions that hugged me. I figured that this couch was older than my nephew, possibly even older than me, and hadn't survived this long without being treated with total respect. I was also aware of the need to not get too comfortable with my thoughts of Lawrence Pixley in public. My flushed cheeks would be a dead giveaway.

Thankfully, Ernest appeared to be oblivious to my reddening complexion. "Indeed, he is effervescent, and the school is in very great need of a makeover. I'm sorry we skipped mass this morning. Just a little under the weather, you know. I don't like to miss a service, but that hall gets so cramped. Wouldn't want to spread my germs to the entire congregation."

"I'm sure God will understand."

"Yes, let him be my judge. Now, Reverend Ward, I'm sure you haven't just popped by to check up on our health." Ernest took up his seat in the smaller of the two leather chairs.

"Well, I am concerned about how you're both feeling following the death of Professor Cheadle."

Tom returned with a gilt-edged tray, three sets of bone china plates, cups and saucers and my sister's carrot cakes beautifully arranged on a matching tiered cake stand which he carefully placed on the glass coffee table in the centre.

"Reverend, I won't pretend I'm overly upset at the news. He was a vile man. Pomposity incarnate. It's no major loss to the world. I hope his blood hasn't permanently stained the flagstones." Tom seated himself on the taller brown chair and folded his arms. He stared at his partner with a look that dared him to counter what he had just said.

Ernest remained silent.

"I think the police will send in a special clean-up team to deal with stuff like that, and hopefully soon." I bit into one of the cake squares. *Rosie, your culinary skills are really improving!* "Has Inspector Lovington been over to ask you any questions yet?" I asked.

"No, why do you think he will? Are we suspects? Surely not!" Tom unfolded his arms and slapped both hands down on his legs so hard, it must have stung a little. Yet he continued, unperturbed. "I mean, I hated the man with a passion, but they can't suspect for one minute that I or Ernest would ever kill him, especially Ernest. As you said yourself, Reverend, Ernest was a saint around that man." Turning his attention away from me, he added, "Lord knows, he didn't deserve your forgiveness or your kindness."

I followed Tom's gaze to see a greying shadow where once sat the man we called Ernest. It was as if someone had siphoned off all his inner light. There was clearly more to Ernest's pain than I could understand.

"Still." Ernest's eyes brimmed with water, which he shook out with a blink and a decisive shake of his head. "No one deserves to die like that. No one."

Deeming it prudent to change the subject, I wanted to know more about the May Day parade and what I had missed. Tom gleefully provided a more colourful and detailed commentary of the event than anything I had gotten from my family to date.

"There was no real contest for the Queen of the May. I admire how some parents are willing to indulge their children, but there were a few who one can only describe as borderline delusional! Take the Fletcher child, please!" Tom pursed his lips into a wry smile, which he flamboyantly swept away with a linen napkin. "I mean seriously, that poor lamb would have featured higher in the island's annual pig race!"

"Tom!" Ernest was quick to chastise him, but I noticed a fleck of laughter. "That's a slight exaggeration."

"See, see, *slight*! You agree! Don't pretend you didn't think the same thing." Tom was triumphant. "I'm not cruel. Just honest. If it wasn't for fair Tilly, we would have been the laughing stock of the county."

"The county?" I didn't realise that this decision would go any wider than Wesberrey.

"Yes, all the villages put forward their queen to compete for the county crown on Whit Sunday. The various parishes take it in turn to host the event. Ernest, who is leading the festivities this year?"

"That will be All Saints. I think Tilly has an excellent chance." The animated conversation was bringing the colour back to Ernest's cheeks. I imagined that such gossip about the local community regularly provided their evening's entertainment. "Quite the prize this year, I had heard a cash gift of a thousand pounds for the winner and lesser amounts for the two runners up."

So that would explain Tilly's desire to win.

"I'm calling it now!" exclaimed Tom. "Tilly will dance rings around her rivals. I believe your aunt was the last Wesberrey queen. She is somewhat of a legend."

Ernest rubbed his white moustache as if it held the magic memory genie. "Yes, I believe Pamela won in the early sixties. 1962, if my memory serves."

"Pamela?" *Beige, cardigan-wearing Auntie Pam?* "Surely you mean Cindy?"

"No, no, definitely Pamela Bailey. I think Cynthia Bailey was our queen a few years later, but she didn't win the overall crown." I didn't expect Ernest to have such an encyclopaedic knowledge of Wesberrey's May queens.

My family was a constant source of amazement.

"It surprised me to see Sebastian at the parade though, given that his mentor had been so brutally dispatched the night before?" Tom pondered as he lifted the teapot to pour us all a second cup.

"DeVere was there?" I admit, it also shocked me.

"Well, it was all going on outside the Cat and Fiddle. I can't imagine there was much respite inside the pub. Maybe all the festivity was a welcome distraction," Ernest suggested.

"Perhaps, though he didn't appear to be that cut up about things." Tom offered a bowl of sugar cubes, which I declined. "There was another thing that puzzled me. He was wearing brown shoes." Tom regarded us both with an expectant look, annoyingly for him we couldn't understand the problem.

I was the first to crack. "Brown shoes?"

"With a black belt!" Tom almost exploded with frustration. "And a silver buckle! That is never a good look, ever."

"I imagine he wasn't thinking straight." I have no eye for style. "As you said, it was probably a struggle for him to take part at all. Given the chain of events, how important is the colour of your belt?"

"For a man like DeVere? It is everything!"

Cats and Curried Lentils

I spent a comfortable hour with Tom and Ernest, who proved to be in no hurry to get rid of me once we moved the conversation on from the death of Ernest's former colleague. I didn't want to believe that either of them could be responsible for his untimely demise, but a good detective can't just rule out suspects because they appear to be good people. They were not just good people; they were my friends. Through my divine gifts and the help of, as Poirot would say, 'my little grey cells', I would help track down Norman's assailant. Inspector Lovington was probably joining us for dinner, so I would hopefully get some more clues from him.

Turning up the path towards the vicarage, I spied a familiar figure crouched down by the sycamore tree.

"Lawrence? Is that you?"

Stretching himself back up, he half turned to greet me. A ginger cat draped itself over one arm, others were milling around his feet.

"I made some friends whilst I was waiting." He grinned.

"You like cats, then. Funny, I thought you would be allergic." I said. *Way to go, Jess! Nothing screams 'I fancy you' to a man like pointing out his most unattractive habit.* "The sniffing." *Stop it!* "You do that a lot." *Shoot me now!*

"Oh, right, yes, I do. But for dust, well actually dust mites. And horsehair. Tree pollen as well. But, for some reason, I am good with cats. And dogs. Seem to be okay with the class gerbils as well."

"Quite the collection, then. I'm allergic. To cats, that is. I have to take antihistamines every day since Hugo adopted us. Makes it easier to look after these guys too. The one you have there, Luke named him Felix. And the white female claiming your left leg is Paloma."

Using Felix as a shield, Lawrence drew closer. "I was waiting to see you. I had hoped that perhaps we could have grabbed some lunch earlier, but you disappeared. Barbara said you were probably visiting Tom and Ernest. I didn't think you would be this long."

"Sorry, you should have knocked at the vicarage, Mum would have let you in. Or sent a text?"

"It's okay, honestly. The views from here are incredible, don't you think?" He moved down to my right and breathed in the stunning hills, vales and bays of the western half of the island. The afternoon sun cast a temporary halo around his blond crown, which glowed like a Renaissance saint's portrait. Then the sun disappeared behind a cloud.

"Yes, breath-taking!" I sighed.

Now, Jess, now. I reached out to take his cat-free hand. "Lawrence?" I positioned myself downhill to maximise the doleful look I used to draw men in with, in my younger days. "I'm touched that you waited. It's very sweet." I added, coyly looking up, and trying to ignore the rim of my glasses blocking his direct gaze. *Flutter eyelashes.*

A pause.

A smile.

I bit my lower lip.

Kiss me.

His head tilted towards me.

A scratch.

A cry.

Darn cat!

Ouch! Felix's claws dragged out my flesh and drew blood. Lawrence dropped him to the ground.

"Jess, are you okay? I'm so sorry. Here, give me your arm. I'll get you inside. We need to get that cleaned up straight away."

*****

"This is going to sting..." Mum dabbed some antiseptic cream on her little finger and gently dabbed my wounded cheek. "Good thing you wear glasses or that creature would have had your eye out!"

Lawrence was extremely apologetic. I was terribly disappointed. *Ow, that smarts!*

Mum loved playing nursemaid. "Mr Pixley, you must've had quite the fright yourself. Would you like to stay for supper? I have cooked enough to feed the five thousand. Zuzu said that Dave will join us in a while. The police are just finishing up at the church. Packing up in time for the last ferry. Nasty business, eh Mr Pixley?"

"Yes, Mrs Ward. Terrible. And, please call me Lawrence. As for supper, I would be honoured, if you're sure you have enough. Is there somewhere I can clean up?"

Once Lawrence was safely out of earshot, Mum began her interrogation. "I wonder how long he was waiting? Good thing you came straight back. Poor thing. Think he really likes you, Puddin'."

I winced. "Shh, Mum, don't call me that. He might hear!" My cheeks were on fire. Given my age, there was relief it was from embarrassment and not 'The Change'. I enjoyed the sensation. It was as if there was a permanent giggle in my chest, waiting to break free. And unlike my recent crush on the Inspector, I was certain Lawrence reciprocated. My only negative thought was why did it take me so long to realise? *Give yourself a break, Jess. You have only known him for four months!*

*****

To honour our guests, we ate in the dining room and used the good china, namely a set of floral and green 'Georgian' gilt-edged crockery that looks authentic to the period of the vicarage but was actually mid-twentieth century. Vintage, not antique, but still very fancy. Dinner was a wonderful lentil curry dhal with moreish side dishes of sag aloo, naan bread and mushroom rice pilaf, and Mum *had* cooked enough to feed an army.

To even out the gender mix, Mum and Rosie sat at opposite ends of the dining table, whilst Zuzu and I sat diagonally opposite each other facing our respective partners.

"So, Dave." I was curious. Normally when the inspector has to stay overnight on an investigation, he stays at the Cat and Fiddle. "Are you sleeping at the pub?"

"Er, no Jess, given that the murder victim and Sebastian DeVere have rooms there, I thought that would be problematic, so I'm actually staying in your aunt's spare room." Dave dipped the edge of his naan bread into his curry sauce, "Cynthia has been very kind to give me a place to rest my head. Though being honest, I've hardly been back there. What with dealing with the forensics team and interviews." He brought the bread to his lips and then had another thought, "By the way, Phil kindly agreed that I could set up an incident room in the hall, so PC Taylor has been busy setting that up all afternoon. At least you can have the main church back now, we have processed all the evidence."

"Of course. That's an efficient solution." *And very handy...* "Poor PC Taylor, another murder on his normally quiet patch. I hope he gets some sleep tonight, or do you have him posted on sentry duty in the hall overnight?"

Dave had to finish chewing before answering me. "We locked the place up and you have an alarm system. Phil showed me. I am sure everything will be safe till morning. This is delicious, Beverley. You're all really embracing this vegan thing."

"Wouldn't want to be hypocrites," Rosie answered on my mother's behalf. "I'm feeling so much healthier without milk and dairy and Mum, have you noticed Luke's acne seems to have cleared?"

"I have, dear. By the way, where is Luke this evening?" The formality of her conversation matched the environment. It was like dining on the set of 'Above Stairs'. *'I believe the young master is unavoidably detained at his club, M'lady'*. Master Luke was probably still celebrating with Tilly.

Rosie bristled. "I have no idea, Mother. Perhaps the inspector can enlighten us?"

"I was expecting him to be here. I haven't spoken to him since Saturday morning. He was heading off to the parade." Dave replied, washing down his last mouthful of bread with some wine.

"Yes, he arrived at the school around midday." Lawrence finally found a way into the conversation, "He was hanging out with that young lady who was crowned queen and a few other teenagers from the new estate." Spotting my sister's mood darkening, he added. "They appeared to be in good spirits."

"Don't worry, Rosie, I can speak to him about his statement tomorrow," Dave said reassuringly.

"I wasn't worried about that!" Rosie snapped. "As long as he doesn't get her pregnant."

"Well, it wouldn't be the first time the Queen of the May got knocked up..." Mum muttered into her pilaf.

Pamela?

"Mum, I didn't know that Aunt Pam was once Queen of the May. Cindy, too. Did you ever enter?" I asked.

Zuzu's eyes darted from their near-permanent observation of her man to our mother and cooed in anticipation of some juicy family titbit. "Jessie, what are you saying? Pamela! Mum? Did she get pregnant?" The possibility that Zuzu wasn't the first 'fallen woman' in our history was a family secret my sister wasn't about to let go of easily. "I mean, we all know, family goddess legend and all that, that Cindy has never been pregnant, so unless it was you."

"I never flaunted myself in that stupid parade." Mum scowled.

Lawrence leaned in and whispered to me, "Goddess legend?"

"I'll explain later." I mouthed back, putting my finger on my lips. Any school teacher would recognise the universal signal to stop talking. Lawrence obediently retreated into his chair.

I didn't have time for family secrets. As soon as dinner was over, I was going to take a peek inside the evidence room.

Arise, Sir Luke!

T he gentle night air wrapped around me as I waved Lawrence off into the night. A pleasurable evening ended with a tender kiss and the warm promise of an actual date next time. I lingered in the doorway just long enough to ensure that he was safely out of sight before lifting my coat and hat off the hook in the hallway. I grabbed a torch from the cabinet and closed the door behind me.

I had thought about asking Lawrence or one of my sisters to join me, but Zuzu was so loved up with the inspector I wasn't sure if I trusted her not to tell him. Rosie was obviously too stressed, and I wasn't confident enough in my new relationship with Lawrence. No, this was something I had to do by myself. And that was the plan right up to the moment I spotted Luke trying to sneak back into the vicarage through the back gate.

"Master Luke returns from his adventures, I see." I joked as I snuck up behind my nephew.

His eyes stared back at me, as wide as the moon. "Aunt Jess, what are you doing out this late?" Glancing at the back door, he added, "I didn't want to disturb anyone."

"Don't worry, I won't tell. Though your mother may have something to say in the morning. You didn't come home last night, did you?"

"I am eighteen!" He stomped. "Anyway, you didn't answer my question. What are you doing here?"

I paused. Given that on the last two occasions I was in the church I fainted, perhaps it would be sensible to have an accomplice. This was a genuine test of familial loyalty. If I truly believed that my nephew had nothing to do with this ghastly murder, then why not tell him of my plans? *Trust your intuition.*

"Luke, can I trust you?" I took his hands and closed my eyes. If he had something to do with this, surely I would sense it, somehow.

"Aunt Jess, what are you doing? Of course, you can trust me."

I took a deep breath and quietened my mind. *Listen to your heart.* A smile tugged at the corners of my mouth and the warmest of feelings stirred in my chest. There was no evil here, but there was an element of anxiety, some fear which was understandable given the events of the past few days. The overriding feeling was one of joy. Cindy's words echoed through my thoughts. *You are a channel for the divine.* I'm having a conversation with the almighty, nothing more.

I could trust him. "I am going to sneak into the church hall to look at the evidence the police have gathered so far. I shouldn't be doing this alone. Would you stand as a lookout for me?"

Luke pulled his hand back. "I'm not sure that's a great idea. Last time I..."

"Last time you what?" There was something in his tone that worried me. Had I misread the signs?

Luke shrugged. "Okay, I wasn't on my own on Friday evening. Tilly spotted the door was open, not me. She went in whilst I stood guard. She thought it would be a laugh to hide the Venuses or something. That's all, I promise. We just thought it would be funny."

"And she found Norman's body." He nodded. "Why didn't she tell the police?" I asked.

"We were trespassing, weren't we? She didn't do it. She had been with me all evening. I figured I'm your nephew. People would understand if I felt the need to check an open door. No need to say we planned to play a prank or anything."

"Luke, you have to tell Dave the truth and get Tilly to make a statement too. She might have some vital clue and not even know it."

"I don't think she saw anything. She was only in there a few seconds. I heard her scream and ran in after her. She didn't go anywhere near the body."

"Okay, I understand, but... do you want me to talk to her?" I took the slight tilt of his head as a yes. "We can both have a chat in the morning. Right now, let's snoop!"

*****

As we walked the few yards to the hall, Luke admitted he had wanted to be a hero. Save the princess, that sort of thing. Sir Luke defending the distressed damsel from the fire-breathing questions of PC Taylor. It was sweet. Stupid, but sweet.

Not that I was in a position to talk about being stupid. I unlocked the village hall and turned off the alarm.

"Okay, you stand by the window and let me know if anyone comes. Try not to move the blind, as they will see my torchlight. And don't touch anything."

This, I told myself, was real investigating. Just like all those murder mysteries and crime shows on television. I always wondered why they used a torch when they could just turn on the light. This was much more exciting!

There were a couple of portable notice boards lined along the far wall and a few makeshift desks with computer monitors in the middle of the room, attached to the wall by rather hazardous electrical extension cords. I stepped over to the boards and shone my torch across the list of suspects. Yellow index cards had names written in thick black marker and around these were other coloured cards, Post-It notes and the odd photograph.

From what I could make out, Inspector Lovington's investigation so far had centred on Sebastian DeVere and Isadora Threadgill. There were cards with both Tom's and Ernest's names on them, but no other information. Luke's card had a couple of notes. One simply said *'Discovered body'* and the other *'No motive'*.

There were probably statements from Isadora and Sebastian somewhere, if I could find them. One small table had a wire tray containing several cardboard files. The picture of teenage twins beside it told me this was Dave's desk. I pulled out his chair and after balancing the torch on the edge of the computer keyboard, worked my way through the pile of papers.

According to DeVere, he had dined with Professor Cheadle around seven, before having an early night. The notes read that witnesses at the Cat and Fiddle corroborated his story, but no one could vouch for his movements after eight-thirty. Isadora's alibi was pretty flimsy too. She had declined an offer to join the academics for dinner. She had, instead, returned home to catch a Channel 4 documentary on Cornish smugglers of the eighteenth century. With nothing more for companionship than a Bird's Eye roast chicken dinner ready meal and a cup of Ovaltine.

What about Professor Cheadle himself? What did he do after dining with Sebastian? None of the pub witness statements mentioned seeing him afterwards either, but clearly, at some point, he had left the Cat and Fiddle. Why did he return to St. Bridget's? Was he planning to meet someone there? Whether or not he planned to, someone else was also in the church that night. Did the professor know his killer? I had felt anger. Frustration. If I had been channelling the late Norman Cheadle, then I suspect he wasn't in St Bridget's on a whim. He went to meet someone. A someone with whom he had a difficult history, a fraught relationship, a past.

"Aunt Jess, someone's coming up the path!"

"Get down!" I switched off my torch and dived under the desk. In the sliver of moonlight shining through the blinds, I could just make out the crouched figure of my nephew under the window. "Don't make a sound, it's probably just someone taking a shortcut across the graveyard," I whispered.

Luke was right, someone was approaching. Gravel crunched underfoot as they got closer. Then it stopped. The door to the hall rattled.

"Jessamy! It's your mother. Open this door at once!"

Family Council

"What on earth is wrong with you two? Jessamy, are you out of your mind? There's a violent killer on the loose and you're playing Nancy Drew with my grandson."

"How did you know I was here?"

"You're not the only one who picks up on clues. I saw your eyes light up when Dave mentioned he had commandeered the church hall. I am amazed he didn't see it. I suspect Zuzu playing footsie under the table distracted him. Now, let's get you both back to the vicarage before you do any more damage!"

"Mum, I promise I haven't touched any of the evidence. I just read through some witness statements." Even before my words hit their target, Mum was having none of it.

"Home, the pair of you!"

Luke and I sheepishly obeyed.

*****

Once we were back, Mum ushered both of us into the morning room.

"I will tell your mother you are safe. She's been worried sick!"

A few minutes later Rosie was cradling her son's head on her lap as he lay across the settee. No such tender loving care for me. I was being chastised by a mother and sister tag-team.

"Jessie, this nonsense has got to stop! I have to tell the Baron. You're making me choose between my sister and the man I love. Leave this to the police." Zuzu was pacing up and down in front of the French windows. "This is insufferable! Mummy, tell her. She has to stop this."

"I've tried," Mum responded. "Jess, it's like you have a death wish or something." Mum was beyond angry with me. "It's this flaming island. And it's us. This family. Did you know there wasn't a single suspicious death here until we returned? I warned you, Jess. I told you. You've stoked the viper's nest. Opened Pandora's Box. I think we should all leave."

"And go where? Mum, this is our home. It's where we belong." I looked towards my sisters for support.

Zuzu stopped pacing. "Jessie, I agree. Mummy can move back home and we can sell the shop, the cottage. Take our inheritance and start elsewhere. I mean, it's been lovely getting to know Pamela and Cindy and all that. Finding out that we are all a little psychic is kind of cute too, but look what it's doing to you. To Luke!"

Luke sat up and pushed his mother's hands aside. "I'm not going. I have friends here. I'm not leaving Tilly!"

"You'll find another girl. Trust me, with those baby blues you will have girls falling at your feet!" Zuzu was on a mission. It was rare to see her side with our mother. To be honest, it was a scary combination. "Rosie, come on. This backwater is just a staging post. You can rebuild anywhere."

We all turned to my baby sister. "I'm with Jess." She shrugged. "Sorry. I have big plans for the cafe." She plumped the cushion next to her. "Zuzu, move in with Dave. You know that's what you want. You will have your own money once the will's settled and well, he has a trust fund. You're laughing. The man is obsessed with you."

Lifting her head, Rosie steadied herself before turning towards our mother, "And Mum, if you don't want to pack up everything to return here, then don't. We're all grown up now." She stretched out her hand and ruffled her son's hair, "Even this one!" she laughed.

"I want to know more about our past." she continued, "I never felt at home really anywhere else. Always felt like an outsider. I guess I've been a little unsure these past few days, that murder unsettled me a bit, but I'm staying. I think it would be great if we all did, but I understand if that's not what you want."

"But... but, she used your son as a lookout!" Zuzu yelled in response. "Jess is like a danger magnet. Trouble finds her. Gift or no gift. I think Mum's right. Next time, Jessie, next time..." She burst into tears and slumped onto the armchair next to where she had been standing. It scared Zuzu that something bad was going to happen to me. Her concern was touching, but finally, it was my turn to say my piece.

"I came here because God sent me. I have to believe that He knows best. Maybe, I am the next godmother. Maybe it's all one and the same and, whilst I can't get my head around it all right now, I have faith." The best thing I could have said next was to promise that I wouldn't play Miss Marple anymore, but I had never backed away from a puzzle. This death happened in my church. I had to solve it. Or at the very least, do everything I could to help the police with their enquiries. "I will tell Dave everything in the morning. Zuzu, you won't need to take sides."

And don't forget Lawrence. Don't I want to stay for him?

Mild-mannered Lawrence, who was thirty minutes late for our business meeting. I remembered that he never properly explained what held him up. *Jess, stop it.* He was with you by half seven, and all the reports confirmed that, at that time, Norman Cheadle was chomping down on Phil's steak and ale pie.

"*And* I think this thing with Lawrence might work out. I can't give up on that."

Secret Dossiers

"So, when are you taking Luke in to see Dave, then?" Zuzu was sitting in the carver chair at the head of the kitchen table, stroking a purring Hugo on her lap, like a reverse Blofeld.

"Straight after breakfast. I need to convince Tilly to come in too." I replied, scraping some marmalade onto a slice of wholemeal toast. "Do you want some?"

"No, I'm not very hungry, thanks." Zuzu bowed her head and stroked the top of her chin on the cat's forehead. "How's your cheek? Not all puss-tats are as gentle as you, eh Hugo-kins."

"He will miss you all if you move out. Hugo's not a big fan of mine," I said.

"Oh he loves you, he just knows he makes you ill, bless him. So you think I should move in with the Baron? It is a bit cramped with all of us here."

"We've been okay until now. I'm sorry about last night. I understand you're all just worried about me, but I'm a big girl now. I can look after myself."

"Jessie, no offence, but you can't even hold your own with a ginger tom!" Zuzu laughed. "Anyway, Dave hasn't asked me yet. I mean he's really into me. Of course, what man wouldn't be? I have the power," she grinned over the top of Hugo's head. "But, I haven't even met his children yet. Or his mother. He keeps saying he's too busy. I'm not sure."

"Sis, you can stay here as long as you want. I am sure Dave is working on it. He has a murder to solve."

"There's always another murder to solve."

"Well, I could help him..."

"No, Jessie, no. You agreed to butt out." *Well, technically I didn't agree.* "Just tell Dave everything you know this morning and be done, Okay?"

"Okay," I said, though I may have had my fingers crossed.

*****

"There's really no need to tidy on my account." I tried to assure a frantic Tilly who was scooping up dirty cups and plates from the coffee table in her lounge.

"No, I've been living like a pig, whatever must you think of me? Anyway, my dad is due back from London later, and I can't have him walk into this mess!"

An appreciative smile passed from Tilly to my nephew as he gathered up some food wrappers and other papers from the floor. I genuinely hoped, for both their sakes, that Tilly wasn't involved in Norman's death. I needed to convince her that talking to the police was the best option.

"Tilly, don't be angry with Luke, but he told me it was actually you that found Professor Cheadle. I think you both should go to the police, but first, why don't you talk me through it?" I shunted a pile of news articles on the sofa beside me along a few inches to get more comfortable. An interesting headline caught my eye.

'Antiquarian's legacy founded on lies!'

I stretched my neck over to read more. Tilly followed my gaze. "Those are all about Professor Cheadle. I googled him. He had built quite the career out of debunking local myths and legends."

I lifted up the papers for a closer look. "This is fascinating." I noticed the date stamp from the internet on the top of each page, Tilly printed them out on Thursday, the day before Norman's death. "Why did you do this?"

"I google everyone. See, here is what I could find about you." Tilly handed me a slim card folder labelled 'The Vicar' covered in cutesy stickers and ornate lettering. "Open it, I don't think there's anything bad in there. I haven't read anything properly yet. I find something, hit print, and then file them away. I like to decorate the folders," she added.

"So you make a dossier on everyone you meet?" She intrigued me. My folder had news about me dating back to the early nineties, including one review from The Scotsman of my performance of Emilia in my drama school's production of 'Othello' at the Edinburgh Fringe.

✩✩✩✩✩ *Heaven save us from these pretentious student renderings of the Bard! The only honest portrayal was that of Emilia, who appeared to be as bored with the monotone ramblings of Desdemona as we were.'*

Ouch! I had blocked that out of my memory.

"Yes, I find people fascinating. I want to be a writer someday."

"Don't you think googling strangers is a little, I don't know, dangerous? You might find out…" A thought occurred to me, within these papers might be a clue to who wanted Norman Cheadle dead. "And you haven't read any of them yet?"

"No, I have to do the folders first. I decorate them all with artwork and stickers that reflect my first impression. You know that gut feeling you get about someone. I think that's important," Tilly was proving to be a young lady with many layers, "See yours is quite regal. When I first met you I thought purple and golds. But then there also needed to be warm, fluffy elements, so I chose clouds and cherubs. Shades of lilac and rose. And here," Tilly pulled out a yellow folder from a magazine rack at the side of the chair she had adapted into a makeshift filing cabinet. "This is Mrs Threadgill's, more earthy, but still authoritative, so I chose like sienna, terracotta, with a rich royal blue. Her stickers have a more Edwardian vibe. See?"

"May I look inside?"

The folders fascinated me, and all thoughts of hurrying along to the police evaporated from my mind. The answer to the puzzle was probably within these pages.

Tilly hesitated.

"You know, Reverend Ward, you're right we should go to the police." She stuffed Isadora's folder back into the magazine rack. "You're a busy woman. This silliness can wait. I'll just get my jacket." She stood up. Like well-trained meerkats, Luke and I got up with her. "Let me just tidy that away," she said, taking my file and the other papers from the chair. "Just in case Dad comes back whilst we are out."

She put everything in the rack and took it with her as she went upstairs.

Stay Calm and Carry On

"Thanks for bringing them in. We can take it from here if you need to get going. You know, doing vicary things and all that." Dave shook my hand and stood to indicate it was time for me to leave. He clicked his fingers to summon PC Taylor. "Take their statements, will you? One at a time." He buttoned his jacket as he walked around from the other side of his desk. "Reverend, just a word, over here, please... I was talking to Zuzu."

"Dave, look whatever my sister has told you, I didn't touch anything. I only read through *some* of the statements and Luke didn't see a thing. I promise." The bemused look on his face suggested Zuzu hadn't told him anything.

His eye started twitching. The trademark pencil-thin moustache almost vanished in the angry folds above his lips as he tried to contain his frustration. "Right, well, I was only going to suggest dinner tonight at the Old School House. My treat. And ask you to invite the schoolteacher to join us. Like a double date." He surveyed the floor. "Jess, I thought we had an understanding?"

I tried to get him to look at me. "Dave..."

"I'd prefer it if you call me Inspector Lovington when I am on duty." *Oh, we are back here again, not a good sign.* "You broke in here last night after I left, didn't you?"

84

"I didn't break in. I have a set of keys, remember."

"Reverend Ward, I should arrest you for obstructing a police investigation and tampering with evidence. But as you coldly pointed out before, I want to be part of this crazy family of yours."

"That wasn't me! I mean... I wasn't feeling well when I said that before."

"And you weren't well last night when you broke in? I cannot let such disrespect slide. This is my final warning, Jess. If I catch you interfering with my investigation again, I will arrest you. Do you understand?"

"Yup, reading you loud and clear." I figured the only way to walk away from this with any dignity was to brazen it out. "Dinner tonight. What time shall I tell Lawrence?"

*****

I had a hundred and one 'vicary things' to do, but first things first. I realised from Tilly's dossiers that I knew next to nothing about the two prime suspects in this case, both of whom were probably cataloguing Wesberrey Venuses next door. It was still my church, my well, my excavation.

I slipped back around to the main door and walked in. There was no sign of Sebastian. Isadora was taking photos of the boxes.

"How's it going?" I asked.

"Good, all things considered, I suppose. I can't get the image of Professor Cheadle lying there out of my head. Terrible business." Isadora took my interruption as an opportunity to take a rest on a chair at the end of the trestle table. "Fortunately though, whoever did it didn't damage these precious beauties. Not a single one."

Stay calm and carry on. Isadora Threadgill was a walking advertisement for the British stiff upper lip. "Every cloud, I suppose" I glanced over to where only a few days prior Norman Cheadle's body had lain, pooling blood covering the surrounding flagstones. "They've done a good job with the clean-up. You would never know."

"No, just as well, really. I hope you're feeling better, Reverend. I hear you had another fainting spell on Saturday and missed all the fun in town. Delighted to hear that young girl won the crown. She is very sweet."

"Yes, Tilly is an amazing young woman. Did you watch the parade then, Isadora?"

"Oh, no. Not my thing at all and to be honest, I felt it rather bad form considering what had happened to the professor. It's important to show your respect. Feels a tad off being here today, but life goes on and all that. These precious little things aren't going to catalogue themselves now, are they?" With that, Isadora used her free hand to help lift herself off of her chair and resumed her photography.

"I expected to see Sebastian here. Do you know where he is?"

"I imagine checking out of the pub. He was complaining earlier about how it felt like living in a goldfish bowl. You know what people are like here. The poor chap isn't allowed to leave Wesberrey until the police have finished their investigation. So I offered him a room at my place. It'll be nice to have the company."

"But, Isadora, is that wise? He could be the murderer!"

"Yes, Reverend. And with the same logic, so could I. Sometimes you just have to trust, don't you? Whatever will be, will be."

*****

I offered to help Isadora with labelling the finds. I was curious about her impending new domestic situation with Sebastian. On the surface, it's the Christian thing to do, but given the circumstances, it was foolhardy. Isadora, though, appeared trouble-free as she danced around the table taking photos and writing notes. Every so often she would shout across something to write on a chit of paper to place in a box, which I did without question. It was fascinating.

Through careful study, Isadora was identifying slight differences between the figures from the ratio between their hips and thighs to changes in the patterning on their torsos, though for most of the figures there were no engravings at all. They were simple, rustic, probably formed by hand using local clay. There were two wax forms, which Isadora told me that Norman had suggested were later than the rest.

"By hundreds, even thousands of years he said. The wax forms are indicators of more organised religion, rather than superstitious beliefs. He was most intrigued by the bronze figure. Very rare."

I edged the latest chit into one of the boxes. I was wary of touching any of the figures again. The bronze figure hadn't been there when I first looked. "It's all rather intriguing how they can date these small objects. When did the bronze come up? It wasn't here on Wednesday."

"No, well remembered. Sebastian insisted on jumping down the shaft himself that afternoon. Had a mini metal detector gizmo with him. We might not have found it otherwise. It was in a lump of thick black clay, impossible to see in the dark."

The mysterious bronze had a more elongated shape than the earlier Venuses and was more ornately decorated with spiralling lines and circles. On this figure, it was possible to discern three heads or faces, to be more accurate. All bore slightly different expressions and they looked to have their own themed headdresses, though I could not guess at the symbolism of each one. The three faces of the goddess, perhaps. Or the different stages of womanhood - maiden, mother, crone. *Crone is such an ugly word.*

"I imagine this would have been quite a high-status object. Clay and wax offerings would have been relatively cheap, but bronze would have required copper and tin and someone to smelt it,"

"Very well observed, Vicar!" The voice of Sebastian DeVere rolled around the apse. "I was saying just that very thing to poor old Norman at dinner... I'm sorry, forgive me."

I turned in the voice's direction but had to double-take. Where was the elegant form I had met only a few days ago? Sebastian's suit appeared as crumpled as he did. There was no cravat or tie. Just an open pink shirt that appeared to have traces of breakfast around the top buttons. The extended handle of his suitcase was his only means of support.

"Sebastian, I'm sorry, this must all be so hard for you." I ushered him into a pew. "It's well past lunchtime, I'm sure we could all do with something to eat. The hall is off-limits, so why don't you both come back to the vicarage with me. I'm sure I can throw something together."

I prayed to the Big Boss that no one would be in. My family would have something to say about me bringing two murder suspects home.

We pushed Sebastian's luggage to the back of the choir and set off for the vicarage. I was very mindful of being spotted by Inspector Lovington as we passed by the hall. The last thing I wanted was to be arrested for making some beans on toast!

Once safely in the kitchen, I offered my guests warm refreshments and a basic selection of culinary delights, namely the said beans on toast, or eggs on toast. I could even stretch to crushed avocado on toast. After a quick exchange about poached or scrambled, I started breaking the last batch of eggs into a bowl. Since the household had turned vegan, these were the only remaining signs of our former eating habits. With these used, the house would be cruelty-free, as long as you didn't think too much about the leather chairs, silk wall hangings and ivory letter opener in the study. Or the piles of woollen jumpers, hats and scarves in our wardrobes. The repurposed hides, pelts, bones and tissue of hundreds of animals that made up the fabric of this building. *And what about shelf upon shelf of books bound with horse glue? I bet Rosie hasn't thought about that for her cafe!*

Eggs made and toast only marginally burnt, I set out the table. I poured three glasses of orange juice, and the kettle was boiling for a brew.

Sebastian rallied. There is nothing a good cup of tea can't cure. "Thank you so much, Reverend. That really hit the spot. I'm not sure I've eaten since..." He took a breath. "Since Friday. Not a proper meal anyway."

"This is hardly a proper meal. I'm sure Phil would have looked after you in the Cat and Fiddle."

"Ah, the twinkle-eyed proprietor. Charming fellow. Yes, he put food before me, but I hardly touched a bite."

"Well, that is understandable in the circumstances."

"Don't fret yourself, Reverend Ward. I will see Mr DeVere has three square meals whilst he's with me. A pub is no place to mourn. You need comforting things around you. Not to be all sentimental, you understand. Just best not to be in the public glare."

"Yes, and I will be eternally grateful for your hospitality, Mrs Threadgill. The police turned my room upside down on Saturday. Heavens knows what they were looking for. I had to get out. I couldn't bear to see all my things strewn around the room without a care." Sebastian folded the square of kitchen roll I had placed as a serviette. And unfolded it again, purposefully smoothing out the creases. "They have no finesse in their work. For all their white jumpsuits and dusting brushes."

"I imagine they have also been in Professor Cheadle's room. There might be some clues there, I suppose. Like who he was planning to meet?"

"What makes you think he was planning to meet anyone?" Isadora asked.

"I don't know. If he wasn't meeting anyone, then why was he in the church? He obviously wasn't alone."

"But, he mentioned nothing to me at dinner," Sebastian continued to fold and unfold the paper square. "Surely what happened was he went for an evening walk, happened by the church and disturbed some opportune thieves!"

"But nothing was stolen. Or broken. There was no sign of a break-in or a struggle." *Jess, stop! This is interfering with police business. Isn't it?*

"Wasn't there?" Sebastian appeared to know nothing about the crime scene.

"All I care is that all the Venuses were where I had left them when I arrived this morning. Maybe they were after the church silver. Those candlesticks would fetch a lot at auction, I should think." Isadora ran her middle finger along the handle of her empty teacup. "Any more in the pot, or should I boil some more?"

"You know," Sebastian ventured, "I don't suppose you have any coffee?"

"Just what we need to get through the afternoon," I answered and pulled out a jar of rich Columbian for myself and Sebastian.

Houseguests

I spent the rest of the afternoon helping to inventory and pack up the Venuses. Tom had come over after his shift at the Cliff View end of the railway to help Isadora dismantle the cordon around the well shaft and make the area safe.

"It's such a shame," Tom muttered as he pulled up the rope. "Right decision though, Mrs Threadgill, to call it a day. I'm sure Reverend Ward will let us back in here again when this matter is cleared up."

Isadora affectionately stroked Tom's arm. "You have been such great support, Mr Jennings. I will make sure we highlight your contribution in my write-up for the S.H.A.S. newsletter."

"I knew bringing in that man was a mistake," Tom continued. "He would turn gold to lead. I understand one shouldn't speak ill of the dead, but I'm not saying anything now I wouldn't have said to his face. In fact, I did as much on the night he died. No one can accuse me of being a hypocrite. But Ernest is right. No one deserves to die like that."

"Wait!" I put down the box I had in my hand and took a few steps closer to where Tom was talking, "You said you told him as much the evening he died. When? How?"

"When he came up from Harbour Parade." Tom barely blinked. "I was working on the railway. The youngsters rarely like to work a Friday night. Too busy getting drunk or worse. So Ernest and I fill in the empty shifts. Like just now. They start after they return from school on the mainland."

"So Ernest was...?"

"At Cliff View."

"Making him the last person to see Professor Cheadle alive!" piped in Sebastian.

"Other than the murderer, of course," I added quickly. I couldn't believe that neither churchwarden thought this was worth telling me, or the police.

"Unless he is the murderer. They had history!" Sebastian crowed.

Tom threw down the rope. "Mr DeVere, I hope you aren't suggesting that my Ernest had anything to do with the death of your mentor. I'm sorry for your loss, but you should pick your friends more wisely!"

I had to calm the situation. "Tom, no one is accusing Ernest of anything. The whole idea is impossible. But you need to tell Inspector Lovington. It will help the police create a proper timeline."

"Oh, yes, of course." Tom's eyes widened. "I will. I'll get Ernest to call the Inspector tomorrow."

"Why not go right now?" An agitated Sebastian moved to within a foot of my friend, squaring off in a full alpha male pose. "They're just next door. Unless you're afraid it was your *Ernest* who killed him?"

"There is no need for that kind of talk, Sebastian. I think we're almost done here. Reverend, if you could make sure they follow this up, I will take Sebastian back home with me. It's been a long day." Isadora guided her house guest back to the choir stalls. "We can swing by in the morning and finish this off. Just keep the cordon up. For safety."

"Yes, we wouldn't want another tragic death on our hands!" Sebastian spat back at Tom. Then bent down to pull out his suitcase.

I waited with Tom until they were out of the church. "Why didn't you mention this before?" I asked.

"Because Ernest never mentioned it. He must have at the very least said hello to Cheadle. Not that it was newsworthy. People go up and down in those cars all day. But once he heard of Norman's death, I thought it would come up, you know. But he hasn't said a thing."

"Maybe, he's scared. Or in shock? They worked together once. I imagine there's a lot for him to process."

"Reverend, I'm worried about him. At home, he just sits at that bureau all day, looking through those papers."

"Do you know what they're about?" I set about securing the cordon.

"I never look through his stuff. The secret to a lasting relationship is to value each other's privacy." Tom took a few unsteady steps back towards the altar and sat down on the top step. His head fell into his hands. I went over and put my arm around his shoulders.

"Let's go to the police, eh? I'm sure there's nothing to worry about."

*****

PC Taylor was most kind as he took down Tom's statement. Inspector Lovington, it seemed, had gone back to my aunt's for a shower and to get ready for dinner. Which reminded me I hadn't invited Lawrence. With a quick mime to show that I needed to make a phone call, I left Tom briefly and walked to the end of the hall.

"Hi, Lawrence. Sorry, it's such short notice, but we're invited to have dinner with my sister and the Baron. I understand if you can't... oh, you can. Great! Right, well, I'll see you at the Old School House. Seven-thirty for eight. By the way, he's paying, so we can look beyond the 'two for one' offers." *This is a date!*

I got back to the desk, just in time to hear PC Taylor reading back Tom's statement.

"I regret to say that my last words to Professor Cheadle were 'there's a special circle in hell for people like you. I'm sure the devil is keeping your spot warm!' Is that correct, Mr Jennings?"

"It is." Tom pulled himself upright in his seat. "Yes, it sounds horrid, but I meant every word."

"Right, well. If you could just read through and sign here. I think we can call it a night."

Tom fished out his spectacles from the breast pocket of his jacket and took the pen and paper. After a few minutes, he clicked the pen and signed. "There. Done. When will you want to speak to Ernest?"

PC Taylor flicked his right wrist forward and pulled up his sleeve at the cuff, just enough to reveal his watch. "The wife will have my tea on, so I'll come over in the morning." He patted his stomach. "I trust Mr Woodward has no plans to leave the country?"

"Of course not. I'll have the kettle on, Constable," Tom replied.

Before the Dawn

D espite the earlier stern warning, Dave was splendid company at dinner. He and
Lawrence found they had a lot to talk about, which was a surprise. So deep in
conversation were they at one point I doubt they noticed Zuzu and I slipping out to the
toilet together, as ladies are wont to do, to discuss our men.

Zuzu produced a lipstick from her bag and was trying to find the best light to apply the
next layer of war-paint. "Do you want some? This one has a plumping agent. Makes your
lips tingle a bit but it's very effective."

"I'm good thanks, I have some Chapstick here somewhere."

"Jessie, you are hysterical sometimes." We regarded each other in the mirror and smiled.
"Lawrence is rather good looking. You've done well, little Sis."

Self-conscious that my face flushed at the mention of his name, I couldn't contain the
smile twitching at the corner of my mouth. "Thank you, he has a certain appeal."

Zuzu looked at my reflection and grinned. "I was wondering where she'd got to."

"Who?"

"Fun Jessie. This frocked up, dog-collared version is very serious, you know." She ran the
lipstick along her bottom lip.

"I have been a priest for years now. This is who I am."

"No, it's who you think you should be. You need to smile more." Zuzu marked out her cupid's bow with two brave strokes. "There. Perfection!" She stepped back and adjusted her cleavage. "One thing I can say about your school teacher, every other man in that restaurant has been eying 'the girls' all evening, but Lawrence only has eyes for you." She pulled 'the girls' back together. "Time to get to work, ladies!"

I laughed. "Ready then?"

"Ready!"

*****

Lawrence and I held back after dinner to let my sister and 'the girls' send Dave off into the night. I was grateful for us to have some alone time.

"The Inspector is a nice guy. I was wary after our last encounter." Lawrence's hand landed tantalisingly close to mine.

"What, when he briefly suspected you of murder? I suppose that's fair." I pulled said hand away to reach for my wineglass. *The silly flirtatious gestures enjoyed by a couple across a table.* I chased the condensation up the glass with my finger and semi-consciously put the resulting droplet on my bottom lip.

Lawrence took my hand and kissed my fingertips.

I think I might explode!

Instead. I suggested that as it was getting late; it was a school night and all. Perhaps he could get my coat.

He held my eyes briefly, before pressing his lips, one final time, against my hand. "Your wish is my command, Reverend Ward."

Ooh, headmaster!

*****

I lay in my bed thinking about Lawrence and how quickly my feelings had developed. Maybe it was the Green Man. Spring was in the air and, to paraphrase the words of John Paul Young, love was too.

My eyes traced the moulding of the ceiling rose above my head. My thoughts drifted to how the evening had gone for Isadora and Sebastian. Maybe Sebastian needed a quiet night watching television and drinking Horlicks. Maybe they were watching reruns of 'Time Team'. That would be something to bond over.

I could hear Rosie in the kitchen on the phone to her son, telling him to come home straight away. A short time ago, she worried he was spending too much time on the computer. Endless conversations urging him to get out and do what young people do. Now that he was, she wasn't too happy with that either.

Mum had fallen asleep in front of the television with a half-drunk cup of cocoa on the table beside her. I had put a blanket over her when I got in. At some point, she would wake up and go up to her room.

I hadn't heard Zuzu return. Maybe she was spending the night at my aunt's. I was sure it would delight Cindy to entertain the Baron and his muse. As I cradled my pillow, a part of me longed for the freedom to cast caution to the wind, to snuggle up to Lawrence's warm chest instead of a square of memory foam. But that had never been my way.

How were Tom and Ernest sleeping tonight?

I prayed for the shadow of suspicion to move on. In the words of Julian of Norwich:

"All shall be well. And all manner of things shall be well."

*****

The warm glow of the night before sustained me through a breakfast of crisp golden cornflakes and ice-cold almond milk. An appointment-free diary presented the possibility of a morning filled with the joys of admin. First, on my to-do list, I needed to confirm my visit to St Mildred's for lunch on the following day. I had pencilled in the date several weeks ago, and I knew Reverend Cattermole would want to hear first-hand all the latest about the excavation and the drama that followed. It was, after all, he that put me in touch with S.H.A.S. to begin with.

I opened my emails. The life of an Anglican vicar is full of diversity; rituals and community activities, compassionate visits and endless rounds of tea and biscuits, but at its core, as with most jobs, there was a lot of routine paperwork and tedious correspondence. Still, nothing was going to temper my mood.

Though the sun had been up for several hours, the dawn chorus outside the vicarage was still in fine voice. In particular, there was one stunning hawthorn tree in the garden, whose dainty white blooms danced merrily to the tune of the starlings flying to and from their nests. I could see its thorny branches from the study window. Soon the blossoms would fall to join last winter's berries on the ground, replaced by fresh green leaves, and the plump brown fledglings would leave the nest. Such is the order of things. The natural rhythm of life.

The strongest desire to offer a prayer of gratitude bubbled in my heart. Life was good, and it was time to thank the Bossman for all his bounty. I reclined in my office chair and closed my eyes. The bird song provided back-up vocals to my humble thoughts. Love is a marvellous gift.

A thunderous pounding of the vicarage door shattered my serenity.

"Reverend Ward! Come quick. They've arrested Ernest!"

You Cannot be Serious!

The bearer of such incredible tidings was a breathless mass of peroxide hair and 'Liquorice Allsorts' jewellery. Barbara had run from the White House with the news.

"It's true! I was waiting at Cliff View station for Tom or Ernest to open up and when they didn't arrive, I went around to their house to check they were okay. It turns out that Inspector Lovington and PC Taylor got there around nine-thirty to take a statement from Ernest. I don't really know what happened next. Tom was beside himself. He was babbling nonsense about how he pushed him too far, how he should have kept his big mouth shut, that whatever he did, he still loved him. I couldn't get any sense out of the man. All he would tell me is Ernest is being interrogated in the church hall, and you need to come now."

I motioned to Barbara to lead the way and grabbed my coat from the stand. There was no time for shoes. My mauve bunny slippers slid across the path. It must have rained a little in the night, the tarmac was still wet. *This had to be a mistake. What was Dave thinking? Ernest Woodward!*

Backed by the full weight of my parish secretary, I readied myself to knock on the door and demand my churchwarden's immediate release. I raised my fist level with my head and was seconds away from bringing it down with the full force of the righteous when the door opened. Ernest himself stood on the other side.

A familiar voice called out from inside. "Come on in, Reverend Ward. The more the merrier."

Ernest stood back. Barbara and I walked into the hall.

Inspector Lovington pulled out a chair and waved at me to take a seat. "Jess, I thought I told you to keep your nose out of police matters."

"Er, yes, you did." I took the offered chair and fixed a defiant glare on my accuser. "And I haven't. I brought Tom here yesterday to give his statement. I have no other intel to report. I heard you'd arrested Ernest, which you must know is ridiculous."

"And how would I know that, eh?" The inspector pulled up a chair opposite me and sat down, legs wide, arms folded, forehead furrowed. "Seems to me that Mr Woodward here was the last person to have seen Professor Cheadle alive."

"Yes, but you don't think Ernest could have brained a man with a candlestick?" I laughed.

"This is no joke, Reverend Ward." Dave scowled, one squinting eye at my unusual footwear. He turned to PC Taylor. "I think we have everything we need for now. Will you escort Ernest home, please? Oh, and Mr Woodward if you remember anything else, I trust you will bring it to my attention immediately."

Ernest nodded.

The Inspector added, "Miss Graham, thank you so much for bringing the vicar to see me. I imagine you have a million things you need to do."

A bewildered Barbara looked to me for permission to leave. "Go with Mr Woodward. I will be along later." I watched them leave. "Dave, what is your problem? I did nothing wrong!"

"Jess, you didn't mention Tom's statement to me once last night."

"You told me to keep out of your investigation. Not to mix business with pleasure. You were off duty! Ernest wasn't about to do a runner in the middle of the night now, was he?"

"Frightened people do strange things."

"Why would Ernest be frightened?" I asked.

"Because not only was he the last person to speak to the professor, but someone saw him, Jess. I have an eyewitness report detailing the two men arguing in the churchyard."

"Who? They must be mistaken!" I couldn't believe what I was hearing. "If you think he did it, why have you let him go?"

"Do you see any jail cells here?" Dave slapped his hands off his thighs like a pantomime principal boy. "I had to let him go. Taylor will keep a lookout during the day. There's only one way off the island, and Bob McGuire will alert me if anyone suspicious tries to leave."

"Ernest isn't suspicious."

"No, then what do you call refusing to answer questions unless I placed him under arrest? Even then, he declined to talk without a lawyer present. And he's the only flaming lawyer on this god-forsaken isle." Dave was on twitch overload.

"So you still don't know what they were arguing about, even if it was them."

"Oh, it was them. Once we put the cuffs on and threatened to take him to Stourchester, he sang like a canary."

What parallel universe have I fallen into? This is Wesberrey, not Chicago during the Prohibition!

Dave kicked back in his chair. His face wore a very unappealing smugness. "And I bet you are desperate to know what he said." I knew this was a trap. The glint in his eye told me he was itching to snatch that tasty carrot away the moment I asked.

"I'm sure I will find out when the time is right. Now, if you don't mind, I have vicary things to do." I stood up, but Dave edged forward, gently forcing me back in my seat.

"And those vicary things *do not* include talking to Mr Woodward. Do you understand?"

"But he's my churchwarden *and* my solicitor and..." My protestations met an icy gaze. "And I understand." *Barbara will tell me everything, anyway.*

*****

Tuesday afternoon crawled by with little drama. Barbara would be at that evening's Walkers Workout, temporarily rehoused in the hospital's basement whilst the police had command of the hall. With only a month before her nuptials, Barbara was taking every opportunity to get into shape for her big day. Frederico, the former Svengali of the Walkers' fitness drive (*and my older sister's former Brazilian lover*) was renting an apartment thirty miles away in Stourchester. Without Frederico's leadership, though, the group had kept up his fitness regime. Each of us took turns to lead the exercise routines. Wesberrey's answer to the Kardashians, Avril and Verity Leybourne led tonight's punishment.

After an hour of star jumps and squats to '80s classics, the group gathered, as had become our custom, for some freshly blitzed fruit smoothies. After the successes of the group at Wesberrey Walkathon at Easter, the Walkers had gained over a dozen new members. This was most welcome, even if most of the new recruits were half my age and body size. Many were also Avril and Verity's clients at Scissor Sisters, so they naturally splintered off in a huddle at the end of each evening. This left me sipping my glass of mashed banana, grapes and spinach with the more mature ladies, namely hospital administrator, Martha Campbell (who had opened up the conference room for us), my loyal friend and parish secretary, Barbara Graham, and my arch-nemesis and school secretary, Audrey Matthews.

I wanted to get Barbara alone, but Audrey, normally someone who would choose to redo the entire class on a floor an inch thick with broken glass rather than stand for a second next to me, had other ideas.

"Mr Pixley was whistling a lot around the school today. It was quite unnerving, if I'm being honest. Unnatural. Like he's been enchanted." Audrey had this bee in her bonnet about me being some kind of evil seductress, bewitching every man I met with my sexy clerical collar. Though it amused me to think that maybe this time, she was right.

"Lawrence is excited at having some money to fix up his beloved school. Isn't it attractive to see a man so passionate about his work?" I answered.

"I'm sure in time, he will come to his senses." She snorted down her banana and honey yoghurt elixir.

"Would you really rather he was sad, Mrs Matthews?" Martha asked.

"I would rather he had his wits about him." Audrey harrumphed in reply. This sweaty pillar of scorn and gaudy shellac nails stood a full six inches taller than me, but I was ready to defend my honour. She knew. Everyone knew. And I was prepared to fight for my man!

I didn't need to though as Barbara stepped up in my defence. "We all get what you're angling at here, Audrey Matthews, but I've said it before and I'll say it again. You have the Reverend all wrong. If Lawrence Pixley is whistling like one of Snow White's seven dwarfs after an evening of canoodling with the vicar here, then I say God bless them!"

"Just so we're clear, there was no canoodling," I interjected. *Why did I say that?*

"I have this, Reverend." Barbara pushed me towards the row of chairs by the wall. "Now Audrey, if you don't mind. The Vicar and I have business to discuss. I suggest you join the others."

Audrey knocked back the contents of her glass, grabbed her gym bag and stormed off into the night. The other Walkers raised a toast as she passed. Most of the new members had children at the school, and I can imagine few of them were fans of its officious secretary.

As the air settled, Barbara lost little time in updating me about poor Ernest.

"I stayed as long as I could. Ernest wasn't saying a thing, though Tom spoke enough for all of us. Gabbling away. I didn't think one man could have so many words in him. Phil came up before I left. Ernest might talk to him. But I made sure they had something to eat. I'm so worried about them. What is Inspector Lovington thinking?"

"Indeed, he says there's a witness. Someone saw Ernest and Norman Cheadle arguing that night. Hard to believe." I shook my head at the very idea of it. "Tom didn't hold back on what he thought of the professor, but Ernest seemed to be so forgiving. What could have fired him up so? Have you ever seen him angry?"

"No, never. Not so much as a raised word. He can get a bit frustrated with Tom occasionally, but no, I've never seen him lose his temper."

I needed to take another look at those witness statements.

The Lychgate

If I had known that I was going to have to add cat burglar to my job roles, I wouldn't have worn a neon orange top to the Walkers Workout, but it would have to do. I offered to help Martha lock up to give time for the rest of the group to leave the immediate area and then snuck across the graveyard to the church hall. The cloudy sky helped disguise me in the moonlight, just providing enough light to guide my steps. Ahead a couple of tomcats were fighting over bedding rights to the latest female in heat, but otherwise, the coast was clear.

I needed to keep my 'wits about me' as, without a lookout this time, I was on my own. Once inside, I left my gym bag by the door to enable a quick getaway if disturbed and crawled along the floor to the Inspector's desk. The pile of folders in the wire tray was higher than before. The police had been busy. Most of the files contained statements from people who were in the Cat and Fiddle on Friday night, all saying that they saw Norman and Sebastian at dinner, but no one there appeared to see either of them afterwards. There was the one from Tom, confirming that Norman took a ride up to Cliff View before the train closed down at nine o'clock. Then I found the one from Ernest himself.

"Professor Cheadle arrived at the Cliff View stop around a quarter to nine. He made a comment about keeping my dog on a leash. I knew he was referring to Mr Jennings, so I stepped out of the machine room to enquire what he meant. Professor Cheadle made some very offensive remarks about Mr Jennings and walked away.

I have attempted to remain civil in my business dealings and social interactions with Professor Cheadle, but I regret to say that his comments on this occasion made me see red. I am a man slow to anger, but I was tired. It had been a long day. I suppose I snapped. I walked after him, demanding an apology on behalf of my friend. He continued to climb along Upper Road towards St. Bridget's. I could not let his comments stand, so quickened my pace.

I caught up to him at the lychgate. I grabbed his arm. He swung around and spat in my face. I strengthened my grip. He yelled obscenities at me. He called me a sycophantic rube, a fawning yokel, and a clodhopping queer! I am afraid that the last insult was too much, and I pushed him. He squared up, prepared his fists and dared me to 'take him on'. He lurched at me with his left arm. I blocked him and pushed him back again. I told him he was a drunken hustler, a conman, and a rogue and that wherever he was heading to just leave me and Mr Jennings alone.

Then I turned and walked away. I imagine he continued towards the church, but I cannot be sure. I just wanted to get home."

*****

So Norman Cheadle probably entered the church around nine o'clock. Who would have been lurking around the churchyard at that hour? I needed to find the witness statement that placed Ernest in that argument. *Poor Ernest.* Even the very best of us had a trigger point.

One folder caught my eye. One with a very familiar name. Audrey Matthews. I wished with all my heart, well at least seventy percent of it, that Audrey wasn't the witness, but there in black and white was her sworn statement that she had seen Ernest Woodward and 'an unidentified man with white hair' arguing by the lychgate around nine o'clock on the evening of the first of May.

The statement read that she recognised Ernest Woodward because she had known him for many years and she understood it was her 'duty' to inform the police because she was 'shocked' to see him behave in such an 'ungentlemanly manner'. Her statement though didn't stretch as far as to confirm Ernest's assertion that he left Norman alive and well. In fact, Audrey stated she was afraid of getting embroiled in their fight, so she turned around and took the long way back home to avoid any further involvement. She told her husband Stanley about the fight when she got in and he had told her 'it was probably nothing and to keep her nose out of other people's business.' When she heard about the murder, she knew she had no choice but to tell the police what she saw.

That was true, I supposed, and normally I would have supported her decision, but it made things look terrible for my churchwarden. What I couldn't understand though was why Ernest hadn't voluntarily come forward himself? Or why he refused to speak to the police unless he was under arrest? These decisions made him look guilty. As an experienced lawyer, surely he knew that.

I knew in my heart that Ernest was innocent, but how to prove it?

Perhaps there was something here, amongst the evidence bags or the other statements that would help. I slunk back down to the floor and crawled over a few more feet to the tables at the side of the room. I knew the SOCO team had taken a lot of evidence for testing back on the mainland, so I wasn't too hopeful of finding anything useful. Then one of the clear bags glinted in my phone's torchlight. It was the candlestick!

I grabbed the bag and sunk to the floor. The label showed it had been for testing and dusted for fingerprints. They confirmed the blood to be that of Norman Cheadle.

I knew what I had to do.

I opened the bag and reached inside. I grasped the top of the candlestick and closed my eyes.

My heart quickened. *There he was!* The moon was shining through the stained glass, creating coloured squares of light on the back of his white hair as he walked away. *Years of anger and resentment.* I saw the candlestick in my hand. There was so much power, so much rage coursing through my arm. *Anger.* Whack! *Revenge.* He fell. *Blood, so much blood.*

*****

It had felt so real. I was there. I was the assailant, except of course that it wasn't me. As I sat there in the dark on the floor, my body embraced the release. I was no closer to knowing who killed Norman Cheadle, but I had a better understanding why. This wasn't a robbery gone bad, whoever killed the professor did so to right some deeply felt wrong. It had lifted an enormous burden from me. I had no sense of guilt. This was a justifiable homicide, at least in the eyes of the murderer.

Sleuthing 101

I crept back to the vicarage unseen and avoided any tough conversations with the family about why I was late. Mum, Zuzu, and Rosie were watching a movie with the volume turned up so loud there was no way they would have heard me enter, so I headed straight to the kitchen to prepare myself something to eat. As expected, when I joined them, they barely noticed I was even there.

In the morning, I sat down at my desk to clear through my emails again before setting off to St. Mildred's for lunch. There was a yellow Post-It note stuck to my screen. It read:

Tilly's dad's back.

She's invited you round for dinner.

Weds. 7 pm,

Luke

Pretty old school, leaving notes. He could have sent a text. Anyway, I was extremely curious to meet Tilly's father. What should I expect from an entrepreneur who had abandoned his wife and daughter to hang out at dance clubs with his associates?

*****

The ferry to Oysterhaven was unusually busy. The channel, by comparison, was the calmest I had ever seen it. The smooth waters disturbed only by diving seagulls keen to catch their lunch.

Bob McGuire was, as usual, in top form.

"Mind how you go there, Vicar. It's been like this all morning. Out and in."

I commented on the beautiful weather and he agreed it was a wonderful day to be alive, which led the conversation on to the latest point of island gossip.

"Can't believe what they're saying about old Woodward. Can you, Vicar? I have a lot of time for that Inspector Lovington, but I think he's barking up the wrong tree on this one. Though who else could it be?"

My thoughts exactly. Despite all the evidence, I remained convinced Ernest was innocent. Suspecting it may be Tom was an even further reach. I believed Luke implicitly, so it logically followed that Tilly didn't have time to do it. I couldn't think of a motive, anyway. There had to be a motive. Sleuthing 101. So I have two suspects; Sebastian DeVere and Isadora Threadgill. Again, what motive could either have to brutally attack Norman? Professor Cheadle was the renowned Neolithic expert whose views on the Venuses would decide their place in history. What possible advantage would either have in killing him before he published his findings? And I couldn't ignore the candlestick and what I saw.

Felt.

Experienced.

No, Norman's assailant had determined to get revenge for something. This wasn't a random attack, but was it premeditated? Whoever struck the fatal blow coursed with justifiable rage. They felt they have done the right thing, and the world was a better place without Norman Cheadle in it.

*****

Just before Easter, I had spent some time helping at St Mildred's when Reverend Catter-mole was ill in hospital. It was a pleasure to be back here again. The housekeeper, Prudence Beckworth, had prepared a handsome spread.

"Awful news about that academic fella, eh, Jess? Murder seems to follow you around like an unpleasant smell." It amazed me it had taken Richard a full twenty minutes of munching mushroom quiche and coleslaw to broach this topic of conversation. "Messy business being done in by a candlestick, I would imagine."

"Not the most pleasant of crime scenes to witness, no. I could put the blame for all this drama at your door," I suggested. "It was your idea to bring in S.H.A.S. to look for that well."

"True, you know how much I love true crime. Though I don't get as involved as you, dear child," he chortled. Taking a large bite out of a Melton Mowbray he proclaimed, "Mrs Beckworth, where did you get these pork pies? They are to die for! Sorry, Jess, no pun intended!"

"Richard, how well do you know Isadora Threadgill and Sebastian DeVere?"

"Well, I don't know that DeVere chappie at all, but I have known Isadora for... let me see, she used to tag along with her father, Reginald... must be forty years or more."

"Tagged along with her father? Where?"

"Everywhere, they were inseparable. Well, that was until he remarried. His first wife died when Isadora was a child. So tragic. Lung cancer, and that poor woman never smoked a day in her life. She worked at the local newspaper. Maybe she got it there, or in the newsroom, at that London paper she worked for before she got married. Passive smoking, they'd call it now. Different world..."

"Must be hard to lose a mother so young." I couldn't imagine losing my mother. A mother has a special place in a child's development. Even though Dad died when I was thirteen, I doubt the impact was the same. "What did her father do?"

"What didn't he do? He was always up to something. You know the type. Member of the Rotary Club, volunteer at the local animal shelter, a fundraiser for the clock tower, town councillor. He was a very active congregant at St Mildred's. Oh, and of course, founder of the Stourchester Historical and Archaeological Society. Our Group, as it was first envisioned until some wag pointed out the initials spelt S.H.A.G!" Richard chortled into his Darjeeling, prompting Prudence to offer to make a fresh pot.

"A busy man. And he looked after Isadora as well, all by himself. I imagine they were very close." Savouries consumed, I eyed up the chocolate eclairs.

"Like two peas in a pod. Old Bryant doted on his little princess. She was the world to him. He only took a second wife when Isadora went to college." Taking advantage of the break in his thoughts, Richard stuffed a whole eclair in his mouth. He barely chewed! "Shame they never got on. She got married and moved to Wesberrey. Cut them both off. Broke her father's heart. After he died, God rest his soul, Isadora took over the society, I think it was her way to make amends."

"Hmm, I see. And her stepmother, is she still alive?" I wondered.

"Oh, I imagine so. Moved to Stourchester, remarried, I think. Though I doubt Isadora would have much to do with her."

"More tea, Reverend Ward?" Prudence returned with a teapot resplendent in its multi-coloured crocheted cosy. "I can make more sandwiches. And I think there's a box of egg custard tarts in the fridge, if you'd prefer. So lovely to have company."

I declined. I needed to leave some space for dinner that evening at Tilly's.

"I'm afraid there's not much else I can tell you. When she's not waving a metal detector over some scrubland or labelling civil war bullets for the local museum, Isadora works behind some anonymous desk at the council. Been there for years. Probably has a grey cubicle of her own by now. Who knows?"

As I thanked my generous hosts for their hospitality, Richard had one more parting thought to share. "I have known Isadora all her life. If you are looking for murder suspects,

I suggest you look elsewhere. My money's on DeVere. *Se-bas-tian De-Vere.* Sounds every inch the scoundrel to me. Don't you think?"

Young Love

I didn't know what to think except that I was no closer to knowing who wielded that candlestick than I was the night before. Maybe the answers lay in those files Tilly made up. Tonight I had to persuade her to let me look inside.

When I arrived at the vicarage, Luke was pacing up and down the hallway.

"Where have you been? Tilly is pulling out all the stops tonight, and we can't be late!"

"Hush now, nephew! We have plenty of time. You're looking rather dapper. Very handsome." I pinched his alabaster cheek as I passed. "I should take a photo, your mother would love it!"

"Aunt Jess, don't you dare!" he said, trying to grab my phone out of my hand. "Can you just get ready? *Please!*"

I blew him a kiss from the bottom of the hall stairs. "Don't worry. I will be back down as soon as possible. Relax!"

I took a quick shower and then stared for ages at the contents of my wardrobe. What to wear? This was obviously a big deal for Luke and Tilly, but surely her father was not expecting anyone to dress up, unless they always dressed up for dinner. Given that he lived in one of the new-build houses on a modern family estate behind the graveyard and not Bridewell Manor, the ancient family seat of the sixth Earl of Stourchester up the road, I doubted it would be that formal. Still, I had few options outside of black and grey shirts, some lycra workout clothes and a couple of 'special' tops, which I had already worn in the past week. If Lawrence was going to make a habit of taking me to fancy restaurants, I would need to do some shopping.

I finally settled on a black clerical blouse with three-quarter length lace sleeves. I had bought it under extreme pressure from my older sister to liven up my appearance, and it had languished unloved in the entrance to Narnia for months. Thankfully, it fit. In fact, all those Walkers Workouts had worked out. I could have bought this top at least one size smaller. It wasn't too dressy; I was still very much a vicar, but it was more feminine than my usual attire.

As there was the faintest mist in the air and the very strong likelihood of showers later, we took Cilla, though it was little more than a ten-minute walk. Luke sat tight behind me. His nervous heart pounded through my jacket. *Bless him.*

Tilly had pulled out all the stops. The house was spotless. She escorted us into the lounge and offered us some bucks fizz, or rather some sparkling white wine of unknown pedigree with a generous dash of orange juice from a carton. I would like to say this deduction was all down to my refined palette, but the opened bottle and cartons were on the side dresser.

"Dad will be down in a bit. He had a late business call." Luke ran his free hand through his tousled black locks, his feet dancing nervously on the spot as he waited. Tilly stretched out her fingertips to brush his jaw. He glanced up at her when they touched before going back to examining the pattern of her carpet. "Don't worry," she said. "He doesn't bite."

I was so preoccupied with the prospect of getting another look at Tilly's secret files that I hadn't stopped to appreciate what an honour it was that my nephew had invited me to this important dinner/event/occasion. He didn't ask his mother; he asked me. I suppose that took the pressure off him a little, though I failed to see why he was so nervous. After all, Tilly had met the entire family.

"I'm sure Tilly's father is going to love you," I said.

"Hmm," he replied.

Fortunately, his agony was short-lived. The unmistakable sound of an alpha-male descending the wooden staircase heralded Tilly's father's entrance.

"So, this is the young stud who's been keeping my girl warm and toasty when I was away." Tilly's father rounded on my nephew and playfully punched him in the arm. "Don't worry, son." He wrapped his muscular arms around Luke's thin shoulders, "Only joking with yah," The beast of a man then turned his attention to me. "Ah, you must be Reverend Jessamy Ward. Tilly has talked more about you than this fine young man. Something amiss there, don't you think?" He stuck out his hand, "Let me introduce myself, Warren Driver. Most of my friends call me Buck. Pleased to meet yah."

I was half afraid that his huge hands would crush my dainty paws, but he had the softest of grips and an electrifying smile. Buck Driver was a man full of confidence and vigour. I could see how, whatever business he was in, he always won the deal. He had swagger.

"Is that an accent I detect?" *Sounds American.* "I'm sorry, I assumed you'd be English,"

"Oh, because of Tilly here. Hasn't she turned out to be the prettiest thing you ever saw? Don't blame young Luke here, would be hard for a red-blooded man to resist her charms." Buck's hand squeezed Luke's shoulders tightly as he spoke. Luke winced in pain. "But, yes Ma'am, I hail from Austin, Texas. Been living over here now for a quarter of a century."

"Shall we eat?" Tilly valiantly scooped her arm through Luke's, freeing him from her father's clutches. "I don't want it to spoil."

"Sounds wonderful. Lead the way," I answered.

The dining room, like the rest of the ground floor, was like an IKEA showroom. Everything was fresh, functional with soft, clean lines and just enough colour and modern art to make one feel at home. But it didn't feel 'lived in.' In fact, I had the real sense that before Tilly moved in, Buck was rarely here.

"You have a lovely house, Buck. How long have you lived here?"

"Good question, Reverend, I bought the place about two years ago to add to my portfolio. Never really got around to do much with it. Then when Tilly here looked me up, and she was living with her Mum in Stourchester, why I knew I had to open this place right up and make this my base." He beamed as he spoke about his daughter. "Did she tell you she wants to go to college, Reverend? Brains and beauty. Just like her Daddy!"

"Yes, she did. And she wants to become a writer. I think she'll do well."

"Well, she'll have plenty of material for a crime novel living round here. There seems to be a murder every few weeks. I thought I was in Dallas!" Buck's laugh was like being in the hold of a spaceship's tractor beam. Once it trapped you in its field, there was no escape.

He narrated anecdote after anecdote, and each time the volume dialled up another notch. There was little room for anyone else to speak. His performance was at times overbearing, but always captivating. He used charm as a weapon of defence, disengaging his opponent with compliments and smiles. Tragically though, I suspected he saw everyone as an enemy to win over. Everyone.

I finally broke through. "Buck, it must have been strange to find Tilly on your doorstep after all these years."

"Yes, ma'am. She could give that Inspector Levington a lesson or two in detecting."

"Lovington." I tried to correct him, but I don't think he was listening as he rolled on with his story.

"She never did tell me how she tracked me down, but I'm sure glad she did. I had no idea that her poor mother had fallen on such hard times. I mean, I'm sure she did the best she could. I'm in no position to cast stones. Soon as I knew what was going on, I scooped her up and placed her in a clinic. It's a disease like any other, isn't that right, Reverend? It needs treatment. You don't expect to get well without professional help for cancer, now do you? Alcoholism is just the same. I have bought her the best help that money can buy. And when she's out, I will move her in here. Reverend, have you seen the rathole she was living in? And having my daughter there too!"

"I'm delighted that Tilly is enjoying getting to know you after all these years. I hope you don't think me rude, but why did you leave?" It *was* rude to ask, but the shared sisterhood inside wasn't able to sit and listen to another woman being berated for struggling to be a single mother, especially not by the father who had walked away.

Buck slammed down his hand on the table and then laughed. "Hey, and I was just getting to like you!" I think he was joking. "Let's just say that Her Majesty wanted me to stay in one of her less refined palaces."

The penny dropped. "Oh, you were in prison! What were you charged with?"

"No flies on you, Reverend! Don't look so scared, I'm toying with yah. Fraud, though of course, I'm innocent of all charges. I was simply giving the firm's partner's money a well-deserved vacation in my bank account. Just to attract a little interest. They got their money back. No harm, no foul."

"But there was harm, you missed your daughter growing up," I countered. Poor Tilly. I genuinely hoped that this would be the start of a wonderful new life. I thought it was a good time to steer the conversation in a new direction. "Anyway, that's in the past. No point to looking back, is there? However, talking of crimes and punishment, I was wondering, Tilly, if the police had spoken to you again at all?"

Tilly shot a look at Luke and shook her head. There was still something they weren't telling me.

"Luke? Tilly? Is there something else? You know the police think Ernest Woodward did it. They have a witness who says that they saw him in a fight with Norman outside the church at around nine o'clock."

"It wasn't him," answered Luke. "Tilly, we have to tell my aunt what really happened." Tilly played with the cold peas left on her plate. "It's okay. They will understand. Jess is cool." Luke caught her hand and brought it to rest on the table. With his other hand, he curled a stray lock of hair behind her ear.

Tilly sighed. Still fixing her eyes on the plate in front of her, she stuttered, "W-w-w-we were there. We saw the two old men fight, and we saw Mr Woodward walking away. The professor carried on towards the church."

"I don't understand. Luke? Tilly? Why couldn't you tell the police? They have Ernest under virtual house arrest and you know he didn't do it, right?"

"He couldn't do it. We would have seen him." A muscle was twitching in Luke's flushed cheek. It was unusual to see any colour in his complexion.

Buck's earlier bravado had softened, he took his daughter's other hand "So, princess, what were you both up to that you are so scared to tell us?"

She snatched her hand away. "I'm not your princess, I'm a whore!"

"Tilly, don't!" Luke held her tight. Their embrace muffled whatever they both said next.

I gestured to Buck to step away and leave them be.

"We didn't want to come forward because," Luke took a fortifying breath, "we were making love on the tombstone."

"Oh, is that all?" Buck's relief cut a slice through the rising tension, "I thought you were going to say you off'd the guy!" He refilled everyone's glasses. "I think we could all do with another drink!"

"I'm with your father on this, Tilly. You are young, there's no shame in what you were doing." *Well, there was, a little but...* "That said, I would have preferred that you had waited until you got married. But it's not a hanging offence!"

"But we were in a cemetery. Next to a church!" Tilly reminded us.

"In public. Like, isn't it sacrilegious?" Luke asked. "Mum will kill me!"

"Don't be silly, Luke." I smiled, "She will just make you *wish* you were dead, for a week or two."

Buck jumped into the conversation like a grizzly bear into a vat of fresh salmon, "Tilly, me and your mother used to get up to all sorts when we were your age. Why, there was this one particular carnival ride, hoo-wee, don't know how I didn't get hauled off for public indecency!"

Tilly giggled. "Well, you looked fully respectable in that picture on the mantelpiece."

"I proposed to her on that ride, and that darn fool woman accepted. I've brought her nothing but pain and suffering ever since." The man mountain wiped a tear from his lashes. "But I'll make it up to you now, girl. I promise."

Buck reached over the corner of the table to encase the young couple in his extended arms, his fingers stretching to round Luke's shoulder.

I hated to break up this tender moment, but I had questions. Lots of them.

"Okay, just so I've got this straight. You were getting to know each other better when you heard Ernest and Norman arguing in the churchyard. You saw them fight, and you also saw Mr Woodward walk back to his house. Did you see the professor go into the church?"

"No, er, we weren't erm quite finished," Luke answered, understandably bashful in front of Tilly's father.

Tilly picked up the baton. "Luke wanted to walk me home. We decided it would be quicker to go around the side of the church and that's when we, well I, noticed that the side door was open. I thought it would be fun to, you know, go inside. Luke wasn't sure but, well, anyway when we got there the lights were on and I thought Luke would like to see all the Venuses, so we went up to the altar."

"Okay, so that's when you found the body?" I asked.

Luke looked to his girlfriend for support. "Not exactly. Well, not straight away. But ..."

"I saw him over Luke's shoulder," she shivered, "He must've been there all the time."

"So why didn't you call the police straight away?" Buck asked, pulling back into his chair with a glass of wine in his hand.

"I wanted to," said Luke.

"But I stopped him. I was frightened. I have a past I'm trying to forget. I didn't want people to hear that we were, *you know*. It's a small place. People talk. It's not the big city. I want a fresh start. So, I ran home and Luke called the vicarage after a few minutes."

This deception piqued Buck's curiosity. "You called for a priest before alerting the authorities?"

"Aunt Jess, has a, er, gift for routing out murderers. I knew she'd know what to do," Luke explained.

"But I was out for dinner." *Don't think about Lawrence.* I felt my breath quicken. *Too late!* I need to focus. "And you didn't see anyone else enter or leave the church?"

"No, we were a little preoccupied."

Buck placed his glass in front of him and held the base between his thumb and forefinger. The stem was so fine I imagined he could snap it with one tiny flick. "So how long were you *preoccupied*? Five minutes, ten?"

"Maybe more," Luke's earlier bashfulness was dissolving into pride at his sexual prowess. "I wasn't watching the clock."

"No, of course not, son. I understand." Buck was taking these revelations of young lust in his stride. "But whilst you were busy, the murderer had plenty of time to slip away."

Tilly suddenly fired up, her entire body engaged with her response. "I think the professor was meeting with someone," she said. "He wasn't in the church on a whim. This *someone* laid in wait for him. Maybe they exchanged words, or maybe Norman didn't know what hit him. But the murderer wasn't hanging around. They probably went out the side door, leaving it ajar. That's how we got in and there was no one else inside."

"So," Buck continued to roll the glass stem between his fingertips, "the murderer knew the victim well enough to lure him into the church, late at night. Probably offering him something he wanted and wham! Blunt object upside the head."

"Exactly!" squealed his daughter. "But who? It had to be premeditated. Isn't that right, Reverend? They must've had a motive."

"Tilly, do you want to help me solve this?" I asked.

She nodded repeatedly.

"Whoa, slow down there a moment, Reverend. I hope you're not leaving me out of this. I get cons, remember. I was one."

"Of course, Buck. The more the merrier. Tilly, I think we need to inspect your secret files."

The Usual Suspects

L uke cleared the table of the remains from our feast, whilst Tilly ran upstairs to fetch her magazine rack. It delighted me she was so keen to share. I had thought last time that she was wary of letting me see the contents, but perhaps she was just nervous about my asking too many questions. Within minutes the four of us were looking through Tilly's cutely decorated folders, each containing potential motives for murder.

I had picked up Sebastian DeVere's file. It was grey with spots of yellow and gold. There were lots of swirls and Fleur de Lys stickers. "Why the French influence?" I asked.

"Because his name is French. Also, don't you think he has a Parisian air? Like he would have been happier as a courtier at Versailles."

I agreed. Tom, who has an eye for such things, had also remarked on Sebastian's attention to style. Not only was he wearing a black belt with brown shoes, according to Tom, a major fashion faux pas, but he looked more like a tramp the last time I saw him. Was the guilt of his actions eating away at his sartorial soul? Or was it grief? The folder had little to enlighten me.

He had an impressive pedigree, though. Schooled at Eton, his father was something big in antiques and fine arts. There was one article about DeVere's auction house in London breaking records with the sale of a Van Gogh sketch. With a buyer's premium alone of twelve percent, the company made £480,000. His family's wealth explained the Italian suits. But not why he would want to kill his mentor.

"How are we going to review this?" I wondered, "Should we pass the files around and then compare notes?"

"Well, I have the victim's file here and from what I can see there's a pool of suspects we haven't got files for. This man made a living from calling out charlatans and fakes. I'm guessing that made him a truckload of enemies," Buck replied.

We swapped files. Next for me was Ernest Woodward. Whilst I knew that Luke was certain Ernest couldn't have slipped back to the church without them seeing, there was still a possibility that he had. The couple were, as they said, 'preoccupied'. Though every part of me screamed he must be innocent, I couldn't prove it. Ernest's file was also grey but was very formal and business like, much like the man himself. Tilly had drawn cityscapes and used stickers of black umbrellas and bowler hats. The file had a frame around its edge made of a mottled-silver-grey animal print, the only nod to his more eccentric hidden depths.

"Tilly, I have to say you've captured people's essences with your designs and you only knew each of them for a few hours at most."

"Like I said before, Reverend. I like to capture my first impressions. Take the file you're holding right now. Mr Woodward. He appears so prim and proper, but I sensed a different side to him. A man capable of so much love and forgiveness. An artist trapped in a business suit. I am sure he was a remarkable lawyer in his day, driven by compassion and empathy but governed by process and protocol."

"Listen to my girl, Reverend. She even sounds like a writer." Buck radiated with pride. They had had a tough start, but I truly believed they would have a great relationship in the future.

"I agree. Her powers of observation are remarkable. If I were setting up a detective agency, I would want her in my team."

Next up was Isadora. There wasn't much about Isadora herself inside. Most of the articles were about her father. As Reverend Cattermole had reported, he was a very active member of the community. His obituary in the Stourchestershire Times made for interesting reading.

"Reginald Bryant passed away in his sleep, May 1st, following a brief battle with liver cancer. His loving wife, Rita, remained at his bedside till the end. Reginald was known to the people of Oysterhaven as a loyal Rotarian and active town councillor. A deeply religious man, he volunteered at Journey's End animal hospice for over ten years. He is best remembered for his philanthropic nature and his legacy of active fundraising for local good causes. He is survived by his wife, Rita, and his daughter, Mrs Isadora Threadgill."

No mention of his first wife, and more intriguing, no mention of S.H.A.S. I imagined his second wife wrote the obituary at a time of deep grief. It was probably just an oversight.

And finally, I got my hands on the file of the main man, Norman Cheadle himself. As Buck suggested, there were plenty of possible suspects with strong motives. He had built his career on tearing other people's down. There was article upon article spanning over twenty years. Maybe his killer was a hired gun, paid by a consortium of his former victims, who snuck on and off the island under the cover of darkness. Unknown. Unseen. Undetectable.

Only one article linked the late professor with any of our other suspects, but it was hardly a basis for murder. Quite the contrary, this story was about how he secured over two million pounds in funding for a new archive at Stourchester University. They named the benefactor as Charles DeVere O.B.E, of DeVere's Auctioneers.

"I think the butler did it!" laughed Luke, now more relaxed than he had been earlier that evening. "It's always the butler. Or the person you least expect. Maybe Norman Cheadle committed suicide."

Tilly giggled. "Yeah, he bashed his own head in." She sweetly rubbed his hair. Everyone rubbed Luke's hair. He would be bald by twenty at this rate. "My money is on DeVere. He is ambitious. He has the height. Can't see how Isadora would have the strength. And she is so sweet. I doubt she ever would get that angry. Crotchety? Yes. Murderous? No."

PENELOPE CRESS, STEVE HIGGS

Buck shook his head. "I hate to say it, ya'll, but the only one I see having a motive here is Ernest Woodward. There were several reports in that folder relating to the rumour that Cheadle defrauded his legal firm. Though he went on to expose other cheats and liars, as they say, it takes a thief to catch a thief. My suspicions are that he was guilty and all these years later, mild-mannered Mr Woodward lured him to the church under a false name or something and then set up the fight to give himself an alibi. Then once he knew someone had seen him going back home, he doubled back and wham!"

"Hmm, interesting theory," I couldn't imagine my churchwarden being that devious, "but how did he know he was going to be seen or had been seen? People aren't usually lurking around a graveyard after dark." I paused for a beat before sorting all the files in a line. "Hoping for witnesses to give him a false alibi is a high-risk strategy. Ernest is anything but high-risk. Assuming that there wouldn't be any witnesses is far more likely, and yet we know that there are at least three people who saw Ernest fighting with Norman... hmm, how come Audrey didn't see you?"

I turned to Luke. "I guess she was on the other side of the church. Or... it was too dark. There's a streetlamp by the gate thingy with the roof."

"The lychgate. Yes ... and in her statement, Audrey said that she didn't see everything that happened because she took the long way around to avoid confrontation."

Luke tilted his head quizzically, "Aunt Jess, how do you know what is in her statement. Did you break in again?"

"Why, son of a gun, Vicar. You broke into the police records?" Buck appeared mightily impressed.

"I might have strayed on my way back from my exercise class. It's my church hall. Hardly breaking in." I knew I had no defence.

"See, Dad, isn't she something?" Tilly clapped her hands. "When I write my first crime novel, I will base the main character off of you, Reverend Ward."

What's Love Gotta Do with It?

It had been an entertaining evening, even if our real-life game of Cluedo had produced no clear suspect. Between us, Buck and I had convinced the youngsters they had to tell all to the police. Buck agreed to take the couple in first thing in the morning.

Top on my agenda was to visit Tom and Ernest, despite Inspector Lovington's warning, they were my parishioners, and it was my duty to ensure they received the pastoral care they needed at this difficult time.

"Look at me! My nerves are shot!" Tom held out his quivering hands as evidence. "We haven't eaten properly or slept for days. Reverend, we need you to do your sleuthing thing. Have you found anything that can clear Ernest's name?"

I wanted to tell them both about Tilly and Luke but didn't want to raise expectations. Even with their statements corroborating Ernest's assertion that he walked home, leaving Norman very much alive, we can't prove that he didn't go back to finish the job.

"Ernest, what I don't understand is why you were so reluctant to tell the inspector what happened? You must have realised how it would look!"

"I think I can answer that." Tom placed one of his quivering hands on his beating chest, "It was to protect me." He bit his lower lip, rolled his eyes to the heavens and sighed, "I closed up Harbour Parade station around nine-thirty and rode the last car up. When I got home, I found this dear, sweet man crumpled on the sofa cowering in fear. It took me a while to get anything sensible out of him, but once I knew what had happened I, well... I stormed out into the night to find that piece of... you know what, and give him a piece of my mind. Ernest didn't want to give the police any reason to suspect that I had any motive to hurt that vile man. Which I promise you, Reverend, I would've done if I'd found him."

"But you didn't, well you couldn't have. You said you closed up at half-past nine. Then you travelled up. That takes what, five minutes? Allowing for the time it took you to lock up Cliff View station, walk home, find Ernest, get him to tell you what happened, etc. It must've been gone ten o'clock by the time you left the house again. Norman would have been dead an hour by then."

Ernest's mouth twitched into an uneasy smile. "So, it couldn't have been Tom, then?"

Now it all made sense, Ernest thought that his devoted partner had dealt the final blow. His silence was to protect Tom, not himself.

Tom dramatically feigned indignation, "Ernest Woodward, you actually thought me a cold-blooded murderer? I am deeply wounded. Oh, the indignity!" Then he beamed a smile brighter than the Wesberrey lighthouse. "And that, dear boy, is why I love you so very much."

"Well..." I said, thinking that this would be a good time to give the two men some personal space, "I should be leaving."

"Nonsense, Reverend. This calls for a celebration. I'll put the kettle on." Tom leapt to his feet and whirled off towards the kitchen.

A brighter Ernest leant forward in his chair and, fixing me firmly in his stare, whispered. "He would have done it, you know. He was an amateur pugilist in his youth."

"Tom was a boxer!" I gasped. "Well, it's a good thing then that someone beat him to it."

People constantly surprise me. How we change through life. The different roles we play. Our personality quirks and mysterious pasts. Above all, what continues to amaze me is the human capacity to put ourselves in danger to protect those we love.

The brighter atmosphere at the White House made for an extremely pleasant morning. I learnt a lot about Tom's fighting youth. How his father had taught him to box in order to defend himself against bullies and bigots. Turns out he had a natural talent and almost made it onto the Olympic team. A skill Ernest found very attractive when they first met and useful through the years they had to keep their relationship secret.

"I would have easily laid out that sack of bluster," Tom boasted.

"Well, I'm relieved that you didn't," I said, dunking a digestive biscuit into my tea. "There is still the question of who did it, though. I have only two suspects. Sebastian DeVere and Isadora Threadgill. As far as I can fathom, neither one has a motive, but they are the only other people on the island who were connected to him. Neither has what I would call a cast-iron alibi."

"Well, let's examine what we do know," Ernest suggested. "What are the facts?"

"There are several witnesses who can confirm that Norman and Sebastian had dinner at the Cat and Fiddle and that between eight to eight-thirty Sebastian left to go to bed."

"And no one saw him afterwards?" Ernest had walked to his bureau to grab a notepad and a pen.

"But he was at the May Day parade the next day. He was acting as if nothing had happened, but he must have known by then that Norman was dead," Tom added.

"They took his statement earlier that morning. It might have been a welcome distraction. People grieve in many ways." I wished I had been there to see Sebastian's behaviour for myself. Maybe then I would have a clearer sense of how relevant it was.

"And don't forget the black belt! A man like DeVere could get dressed in the dark. He channels style the way other men are conductors for testosterone." Tom's hands danced elegantly up and down. "It's in his DNA. Everything about that look was wrong, wrong, wrong!"

"Maybe he couldn't wear his brown belt..." Ernest scribbled notes, "He was planning to stay a few nights, maybe he only packed a couple of options. One black, one brown. If something had happened to his brown belt ..."

"Like being splattered with blood!" I cried.

"Leather is porous, right? A devil to clean, especially in a hotel room with nothing more to work with than some shower gel. He couldn't remove the stain of the night before." Tom half-jumped out of his chair. "That's it! I've solved it. Sebastian DeVere snuck out of the back of the pub and found his way into the church before Cheadle."

"But how did he get there before him? You didn't see him take the railway. None of the local taxi drivers reported picking him up in town. I'm sure the police would have asked around. Did he have a bike? It's uphill from the Square and quite a risk." Something just wasn't adding up for me. Sebastian was a shambolic wreck when I saw him on Monday. Though, if he were the killer, that would explain why he felt safe accepting Isadora's invitation to stay at her house. "And how did he get into St. Bridget's? Phil swears he locked up as usual."

"Maybe Isadora told him about the side door," Tom said nonchalantly.

Both Ernest and I gasped.

"Isadora knew about the side door?"

"Of course, I showed her."

Open and Shut Suitcase

Tom's revelation certainly put the cat amongst the pigeons. If Isadora knew about the side door, then she knew it would be unlocked and that she could probably creep in and out without being noticed. Whilst there were plenty of potential witnesses to see Sebastian leave the Cat and Fiddle, no one did. As to Isadora's alibi, we only had her word that she was watching television. It would be easy enough to look at the schedules and pick a show that would seem plausible. With most programmes available on-demand through the relevant website, it would be simple enough to watch it later, just in case anyone asked questions.

I was still struggling to work out a motive, but if Isadora was the murderer, then poor trusting, dishevelled Sebastian was in potential danger. I had to speak to Dave straight away.

*****

"Reverend, I have strict orders not to let you inside the hall."

"PC Taylor, I need to speak to Inspector Lovington. It could be a matter of life or death."

"I'm sorry, Reverend Ward, but Inspector Lovington warned me you might try to trick me. I cannot let you pass."

This was infuriating! "Is he in there? If he is, then I can talk to him outside." PC Taylor had positioned himself on sentry duty at an equal distance from the hall to the White House. I could have just run past him if I were twenty years younger.

"As it happens, he has gone to Stourchester. But don't ask me what he is doing there because …"

"I know you can't tell me." I needed to try a different tack. "Well, maybe you can tell me if Sebastian DeVere is still on the island? I have a book on Neolithic votive offerings that he loaned me. I would like to return it." *Just a little white lie for the greater good, the Boss won't mind.*

PC Taylor hesitated. Even though he had just that minute told me that the inspector was miles away, he looked over each shoulder to check before answering me.

"We had a request from Professor Cheadle's widow to pack up his belongings. I have to stay here to keep a lookout. As Mr DeVere is no longer a suspect, he is free to go." *Interesting.* "He will be heading back to Stourchester, so I asked if he could help return the professor's stuff to Mrs Cheadle, and he was delighted. Poor man, he was so grateful to do something useful for his late mentor."

"And to get as far away from Wesberrey as possible, I should imagine, eh?" PC Taylor nodded grimly. "You have a primary suspect then? Come on, PC Taylor. You can tell me, I'm a priest."

"No, sorry, Vicar. The Inspector would have my head." The constable was extremely jittery. Having been on the wrong side of the Baron myself, I could understand why.

"Just a little, teeny, tiny clue. I promise he will never know," I pleaded.

He relented. "Forensics found a set of fingerprints. It took them a while to find a match because they weren't on the system."

"But they are now..." *Think, Jess, think!* "So, they belong to someone on the island that you recently interviewed and processed? And, to my knowledge, you've only arrested one person so far. Ernest Woodward!"

"That's why I'm not supposed to talk to you! I saw you entering there earlier. I am more than able to keep guard on the evidence and watching the comings and goings of the White House. If I see you trying to warn him ..."

"Don't worry, Constable. I was merely there to offer my pastoral support. If Ernest is a killer, then I have no intention of getting in the police's way." *Time to move on.* "Anyway, I need to catch Mr DeVere before he leaves the island. It's looking a tad overcast, I hope you don't get too wet. Would you like me to bring you an umbrella?"

PC Taylor declined my offer. Knowing he was watching me like a hawk, I ran home to pick up Fortescue's Island history to serve as a decoy, then raced to meet DeVere before he got on the ferry. *Cilla is an absolute Godsend.*

Whizzing down towards Market Square, my mind spun with the absurdity of the situation. Of course, Ernest's prints were on the candlestick. He was my churchwarden and was probably the last person to polish them and place them back on the altar before the attack. If the killer had the foresight to lure their victim into a dark church, I think they would have remembered to wear gloves.

I did not know the professor was married. Wasn't it slightly premature to eliminate DeVere? I supposed they were following the evidence, and there was zero evidence pointing at anyone else. At least DeVere was away from the potentially murderous clutches of Isadora. Unless, of course, he was the killer. I hadn't completely ruled that out. He was handsome, debonair and rich. Perhaps he was having an affair with his mentor's wife? That would explain what I had experienced in my visions. If Norman found out, he would be in a venomous mood, and if the affair had been going on for a while that could explain the desire to kill him. It was a long-held emotion. But such a motive would stem from lust, love or passion, not revenge. It didn't feel right.

I parked outside the Cat and Fiddle and rushed past Phil and Barbara, who were clearing up after the lunchtime service.

"Is Sebastian DeVere still here?" I called across, dodging tables and chairs to get to the stairs at the back of the saloon bar.

"Yes, Reverend," Phil laid down his dishcloth. Out of the corner of my eye, I could see his fiancée coaxing him to follow me. "I'll, er, come up with you."

We bounded up the stairs, getting terribly out of breath in the process. I truly hoped that DeVere wasn't the murderer. He could push through both of us panting wrecks without breaking a sweat. Outside Cheadle's room, we took a moment to compose ourselves, then Phil knocked on the door.

"Mr DeVere? Phil Vickers 'ere, may I ask you a quick question about your bill?" Phil added a theatrical pantomime wink for added effect.

The door opened. "Mr Vickers. Reverend? How nice to see you both. Please come in."

"Sebastian, I hope you don't mind this intrusion." I began, "I have this book, you see, and I thought you might be able to answer a few questions." I handed over Fortescue's history. Fortunately, I had skimmed it a couple of nights ago and knew some of its content. "There is an early chapter talking about the siting of the triple wells and I thought it might give us some clues where the third well is located."

Sebastian flicked forward a few pages. "Algernon Fortescue, I see he was one of your predecessors. Probably one of those Victorian historians who recycled a lot of old wives' tales as fact. I doubt there is much here to help, but I can take it with me and explore his findings a bit further if you'd like. I haven't got time now, I'm afraid. I have to get back to work. We've had a junior PhD student covering Professor Cheadle lectures and..." he swallowed whatever he was going to say next and went back to his packing. "I need to get his belongings back to his wife."

"Yes, yes, I understand. Poor woman, what a terrible ordeal for her. And for you, of course, losing someone you worked with so closely. You must have got to know Mrs Cheadle very well."

I watched his face closely for a reaction. There was none.

"He was like a father to me. A better one than my actual father," he mumbled into Cheadle's open suitcase.

"Your father would be Charles DeVere? I understand he recently made a very generous donation to the university." I needed to get Sebastian to open up.

"Papa's answer to everything. Throw money at it." Sebastian collapsed on to the side of the bed. "I'm sorry, Reverend. Mr Vickers. I'm really not feeling up to talking right now. If I could ask you to leave. I'll settle the bill on my way out."

I looked to Phil, who edged back towards the hall. "I understand, Mr DeVere. I was just wondering how you found your time with Isadora Threadgill? Very generous of her to invite you in, given the situation."

"Yes, yes, it was."

I waited for Sebastian to say something more, but he just carried on with the packing, which was mainly books and papers. There were very few clothes.

"I suppose it's a blessing Mr Cheadle brought few personal items. He obviously wasn't expecting to stay long."

"He wasn't one for clothes. If he ever forgot something, he knew he could trust me to have whatever he needed." Something just triggered him. Suddenly Sebastian hunched over the end of the bed, sobbing hysterically. I walked around and perched beside him, stroking his back for comfort. "What must you think of me, Reverend? All this," he gestured to the clothes he was wearing, "is a facade. I don't have his wit, his intellect. I am little more than a clotheshorse with a doctorate in old things. He had the mind. The ability to deconstruct theories and myths. He put the past on trial. And the best I could offer to support his genius was to lend him my jacket or belt."

"Your belt? Sebastian, did you lend him a brown belt whilst you were here?"

Sebastian sniffed, took out a silk handkerchief from his breast pocket, and dragged it across his face. "Yes, not that it brought him good fortune. He was wearing it when he died."

That explains why Sebastian had to wear a black belt to the May Day parade. I sat with him for a short while longer, then motioned to Phil that we should take our leave.

"I will probably visit the university soon," I said. "I have a friend who works in Animal Science, Frederico D'Souza. Do you know him?"

Sebastian shook his head. "No, but then it's a completely different faculty."

"Of course, may I pop by for a visit when I am next there? It would be good to see what you can find out about the third well."

"It would be an honour. Thank you all for your hospitality. I'm sorry if I appear rude, but I need to gather up Norman's things. I'm not looking forward to taking them back to Rita. That poor woman. Widowed again. Her third marriage, I understand. Some people have no luck in love."

Rita? Now, where had I heard that name before?

Checkmate

As I predicted, the heavens had opened. I pictured a stoic PC Taylor standing firm with only the roof above the church gate for protection. I might need his help to question Isadora if only I could convince him to listen to me. Just before we left, I had asked Sebastian if he knew where Isadora would be. His reply? St. Bridget's. They had finished documenting all the finds and had resealed the well. Isadora had arranged for some local labour to move the font back into place that afternoon.

As Cilla and I cornered the top of Abbey Hill Drive into Upper Road, we met with a blizzard of apple blossoms. Wet petals on the tarmac made Cilla skid one-eighty degrees, throwing my front wheel into a nearby privet hedge. I tried to reverse out, but we were stuck. My adrenalin was now in overdrive. I had no choice but to continue on foot. This little 'April shower' was turning into a full-on storm. If PC Taylor had accepted my offer of an umbrella, it would offer little protection now.

I pushed on up the incline towards the church. Some welcome, but equally bedraggled forms appeared on the horizon.

"Weather caught you out as well, Reverend?" Buck led the party, with Tilly and Luke bringing up the rear. "We thought we'd mosey on down to the market. Get some fresh vegetables for tonight's dinner. I think we might turn tail and make do with whatever's in the freezer. You're welcome to join us again. Maybe play more real-life Clue. My money's still on the churchwarden."

Of course, for Buck, this was all a game, but perhaps he could still be useful. He seemed the kind who'd want to assist a damsel in distress.

"Buck, I had a bit of an accident with my scooter. She's at the end of the road in a hedge. I tried to free her from the branches but... Would you be able to take a look?"

"Yes, Ma'am." He playfully slapped Luke across his shoulder blades. "I'm sure we can wrestle her free. So where are you heading now?"

"Oh, to the office, so to speak. I have an appointment at the church and I'm running late." I braced myself to continue the battle with the wind and waved goodbye.

Forging through the final few yards, I wondered how to best approach PC Taylor. An offer of tea perhaps, or a simple statement of my intention to confront a killer. All such thoughts were in vain as I got to the lychgate. The constable was nowhere to be seen. *Probably had to answer a call of nature.* I took full advantage of his absence to sneak into my church unmolested.

Isadora was calmly sitting at the front of the choir stalls reading a book.

"Mrs Threadgill, so glad I caught you. I bumped into Sebastian DeVere in town. He mentioned you would be putting the font back this afternoon."

"Reverend. Is it raining outside? You look soaked to the skin. Funny isn't it how one can be totally unaware of what's going on in the outside world from here."

"Yes," I took off my jacket and tried to shake off some of the water. Then I remembered I still had my helmet on. "Do you mind if I wait with you? It'll be good to see everything back in order."

"Be my guest," she gestured to the presider's chair on the altar. "It is your church."

I chose instead to position myself on the opposite stall. "The past few days have been quite the rollercoaster. I hear the police are close to making an arrest."

"So, I believe. PC Taylor was telling me all about Ernest Woodward. Poor Mr Jennings. I feel for him, I really do. We worked well together. He has a ready wit. Of course, if I had known about the rivalry between Professor Cheadle and Mr Woodward, I would never have invited the university in."

"Are you so sure it was Ernest?" I rested my folded jacket beside me on the wooden seat, placing my helmet on top. "It could have been Mr DeVere? He had the opportunity, and many people hate their bosses."

"Enough to kill them? I don't think so, Reverend." Isadora shook her head and calmly placed the book on her lap. "Well, I think the police know what they are doing unless you have any other theories you want to explore."

There was something about her demeanour that unnerved me. Like she was waiting for me to accuse her. That somehow, she knew I knew it was her, and she wanted to find out how.

The clues were there, of course, she had almost given it all away when she said she couldn't get the *image* of Cheadle's dead body out of her mind. *I should have spotted that.*

"I know it isn't Ernest Woodward," I replied.

"Why, because he's your friend? Or because he is a lawyer and a fine upstanding pillar of the community?" She brushed a speck of fluff off her corduroy slacks. "Appearances are so important; don't you find Reverend? How people see us and the image we want to project. The loving parent, the learned academic, the doting wife, the caring priest."

"Ernest is my friend. And we both know he didn't kill Norman Cheadle."

"Really? Do we? Let's explore the facts. Cheadle swindled him out of a great deal of money. He was the last person seen talking to the deceased and, I believe, the *facts* show his fingerprints are on the murder weapon. Motive, means, and opportunity." *PC Taylor must have told her everything.*

I didn't answer. Isadora was playing with me. Like a cat plays with a mouse before the fatal pounce. The corners of her mouth suggested that she was enjoying her little game. Her eyes, though, offered no emotion.

Silence reigned for several minutes. Both of us caught in a game of mental chess. It was my move next. I had to be sure. Work out all her possible defences. My gut was telling me this was something to do with her father. *Rita!* That was her stepmother's name. *Don't the police do any background checks?* Sebastian said Norman was her third husband, but what number was Reginald Bryant and is there a connection? *Think, Jess, think!*

"You wanted to avenge your father!" It was time to trust my visions.

"Very good!" Isadora looked impressed and fortunately didn't ask me to expand on my theory. "It was just the perfect storm. When you invited S.H.A.S. to dig up the old well, it all fell into place."

I took a stab in the dark. "Your stepmother, she married the professor. That was the ultimate betrayal, wasn't it?"

Given Norman Cheadle's knack for exposing fakes and frauds, my suspicions were that he had something to do with there being no reference to S.H.A.S. in Reginald's obituary. The 'loyal Rotarian and town councillor' had been denounced as a cheat only for his 'loving wife' to hook up with the man who exposed him, after his death.

"They deserved each other. She took my father away from me."

"So, you took her husband away from her."

Isadora sneered. "She'll find another. It's her only real talent."

I thought back to the snippet of conversation I'd overheard between Norman and Sebastian earlier that dreadful day. Norman thought there was a problem with the bronze figurine.

"Did you plant the bronze to test him, or just to draw him out?" I asked.

"My, my, aren't you the clever one, Reverend Ward?" A smug glint lit up her otherwise dead eyes. "When I found the other Venuses, the ruse just fell in my lap."

"What I don't understand is why you invited Sebastian DeVere to live with you?"

"Really, you can't work that out? I am disappointed." She scanned my face. "I have time. You know Cheadle was the victim of his own hubris. I knew he would be arrogant enough to want to confront the fraudster before going public. I willingly gave him his last victory, knowing the key to winning the war was in my hands. Literally." Isadora laughed to herself. A near maniacal laugh that poured itself into the empty void that was her conscience. Stopping when it hit the pain in her core. "You see, my father was just one more charlatan to him. Just another name on his list. Like the Witchfinder General of old, he moved from discovery to discovery, hunting out the innocent and guilty alike. Destroying reputations and legacies." Her earlier calmness laced now with bitter emotions. "When I told him he had unmasked one of his wife's former husbands, he laughed. You know, he said that that was one of the things that most attracted him to her. His exact words were 'to the victor the spoils'."

"And I suppose he didn't connect you were Reginald Bryant's daughter at first. Much like the police have failed to make a connection."

"Crazy, isn't it Reverend, how faceless we women become? Taking on our husband's identities. Losing our family names. I was reasonably sure that he wouldn't discuss his work with my stepmother. Not that I needed to worry, he was so arrogant, he didn't even bother to learn my name. Thurgood!" she sneered, "It was a risk he would remember the Society, which is why I went through DeVere."

"You created distance. Very cunning." And I thought I knew why she offered Sebastian room and board. "You wanted to see if the professor had shared any of his thoughts with his prodigy."

"Marvellous, I knew you would get there in the end." Isadora brightened. "You know, Sebastian is actually an excellent archaeologist. I am sure he will flourish, free of the professor. Now, if you're happy to wait for the workmen, I will be getting along. Things to do, people to see."

She reached down to put the book she had been holding in her bag and then stood up. I hesitated. What was I supposed to do, wrestle her to the ground? She was right; I had no evidence, no proof. As she walked down the steps to the nave and I rose to follow her, she turned.

"No need to trouble yourself, Reverend. The rain's eased and I'm sure that lovely PC is back on patrol outside."

Her words confused me. "Are you handing yourself in?"

"Interesting thought. We can't allow another innocent man to have his name dragged through the mud, now can we?" She paused. "But no, that would be foolish!" Isadora stood in the middle of the church pondering her options. "You want me to confess, because without my confession you have no evidence to defend your friend, and I want to walk out of here unmolested. Let's compromise, I will send my confession through to the police when I am safely abroad. Paris is lovely this time of year, or perhaps Cairo? Who knows?"

I was both incredulous and full of admiration at the same time.

"One thing, Reverend. I slipped a report into Sebastian's luggage before he left this morning. In it, you will find all my father's original notes and the testimonials of several eminent historians who verified that his bronze figure was authentic. There was only one conman here, and it wasn't Reginald Bryant."

I watched as helpless as a squirrel caught in the headlights of a lorry as Professor Cheadle's killer calmly walked down the centre aisle. Immobile. Stunned.

Just as Isadora reached the main doors, one side flew open. The dazzling sun, victorious in its battle with the afternoon rain, streamed through the crack in the portal, casting the impressive figure of Buck Driver into stark silhouette.

It was now or never. "Stop her. She did it. She killed him!" I called out.

Buck dutifully moved in to block her escape. Without missing a beat, seeing there was no way to avoid her fate, Isadora elegantly held out her arm. "So very kind of you to escort me." she curtsied.

And with that, Buck accompanied Isadora out to a bemused PC Taylor, now restored to his post. I caught up with all three of them seconds later by the lychgate.

"Constable," Isadora offered her hands, joining them at the wrists, "Those clouds look rather ominous. I'll make this brief. *I* killed the professor and I'll tell you all about it over a nice cup of tea." She turned and smiled at me, "Reverend?"

"I'll put the kettle on," I answered.

Dinner for Four?

W orld-weary eyes appeared over the top of the menu.

"Jess, dear, are you sure you can afford this? Even with the two-for-one offer, these prices are eye-watering."

"Mum, it's my treat. You do so much for all of us and, well, it's time I treated you like the queen you are. Have whatever you want. The lamb is excellent."

"I suppose it's a good idea to try out the competition. Shame Rosie has decided not to open in the evening, I think it would be a popular alternative." Mum mused as she scanned the entrées. "You know, I think I will have the roasted aubergine. I'm not keen on eating meat anymore."

"Sounds wonderful, I think I'll join you."

We placed our orders.

"Mum, you don't have to answer but, I've been wondering... I was thirteen when we left Wesberrey and yet I don't remember any of this pagan goddess stuff from before. Why is that?"

"Ah, I knew it! There's no such thing as a free meal." Mum pushed herself back in her chair, her arms folded in defiance. I watched the resignation steal away her resolve. Muscle by muscle, her face and then her posture softened. Lowering her arms, she placed her palms face down on the table and sighed. "I thought I could break the cycle."

"What? I don't understand."

She took a few seconds, seeking the exact words she needed to explain.

"There is no greater gift than to hold your own child in your arms. When Pamela got pregnant, it threw us all into confusion. Cindy and I were so sure she was the godmother. When her son was born, that meant the line would fall to one of us. I couldn't believe my luck when your father proposed. He was so handsome." I reached across to hold her hands, triggering them to withdraw to her lap. "His family was so opposed to the match. Whilst they pretended they didn't believe all that nonsense, they knew there would be no male heir to their fortune. I think your father enjoyed that, to be honest."

A lump formed in my throat. I had to ask. "Did Dad ever love us?"

I poured us both some iced water.

"Oh, my dear, of course, he did. He just… He was a rebel. An uncontainable force." Mum tried to take a sip of water. Her lower lip quivered as it greeted her glass. She used a napkin to catch the escaping drops.

"You don't need to go on."

Her eyes darted around the room, searching to find a safe spot to land. "No, I do. You have a right to know." The waiter arrived with our drinks. Mum grabbed her wine and gulped it down.

"When I fell pregnant," she continued, "I knew it would be a girl. I also knew as I looked upon her beautiful face that one day she might be the godmother. That this bundle of love and hope and promise might never be able to…" Her voice cracked. "I thought if I banned all talk of triple wells and goddesses, then somehow it would all end. My family wasn't happy with my decision, but I had to do something. I had to."

"I'm sure you did what you thought was best." I tried to offer comfort, but as before Mum brushed me off and refilled her wine.

"When your father died, that was it. I knew I had to leave this awful place. Give you all a chance to have a proper life. Yet, here we all are. Back here again. Playing happy pagan families."

"Mum, we are happy. And we want you to be happy too."

I wanted to give her a hug. I wanted to thank her for everything she had sacrificed, and all she had done for us. I wanted to tell her not to worry, that I was coming around to the idea of being the godmother and that the most important thing was that we were together. I wanted to tell her I loved her.

"Jess! What a surprise. May we join you?"

Lawrence had brought his mother out for a meal too. *Great minds think alike!*

My mother's relief was palpable. We agreed. Lawrence asked the staff to pull across another table and chairs.

Mrs Pixley was not at all what I expected. In my mind, I had imagined a frail, white-haired old woman, mostly bed-ridden with a pocket full of sticky sweets to hand out to her son as a reward for being a good headmaster. Instead, I was being looked over by a rosy-cheeked former PE teacher, who I was to learn had captained the national women's hockey team.

She threw out her hand. "Finally! Wonderful to meet you, Jessamy. My son absolutely thinks the world of you. Not much of a churchgoer myself. Think it's a load of old phooey, but from what I hear you're a remarkable woman. I understand you're the one who put my old friend Isadora behind bars!"

The End

What's Next for Reverend Jess?

CONSECRATED CRIME

T he summer regatta is in full swing, but this isn't the most highly anticipated event in the local social calendar. The wedding of the year is only days away, and romance is in the air for everyone ... until a body washes up.

Was it a tragic accident?

No, probably not.

Following on from her recent sleuthing successes, the islanders expect Reverend Jess Ward to solve the mystery. But in a race to find the truth, will she be forced to accept her family's supernatural past? Can she crack this case without embracing her own mystical, pagan side?

Find out in Consecrated Crime!

About the Author

P enelope lives on an island off the coast of Kent, England, with her four children and an elderly Jack Russell Terrier. A lover of murder mystery and cups of tea (served with a stack of digestive biscuits), she writes quaint cosy mysteries and other feel-good stories from a corner table in the vintage tea shop on the high street. Penelope loves nostalgia and all things retro. Her taste in music is also very last century.

Find out more about Penelope at - www.penelopecress.com

Want to know more?

Greenfield Press is the brainchild of bestselling author Steve Higgs. He specializes in writing fast paced adventurous mystery and urban fantasy with a humorous lilt. Having made his money publishing his own work, Steve went looking for a few 'special' authors whose work he believed in.

Georgia Wagner was the first of those, but to find out more and to be the first to hear about new releases and what is coming next, you can join the Facebook group by copying the following link into your browser - www.facebook.com/GreenfieldPress

More Books By Steve Higgs

Blue Moon Investigations
Paranormal Nonsense
The Phantom of Barker Mill
Amanda Harper Paranormal Detective
The Klowns of Kent
Dead Pirates of Cawsand
In the Doodoo With Voodoo
The Witches of East Malling
Crop Circles, Cows and Crazy Aliens
Whispers in the Rigging
Bloodlust Blonde – a short story
Paws of the Yeti
Under a Blue Moon – A Paranormal
Detective Origin Story
Night Work
Lord Hale's Monster
The Herne Bay Howlers
Undead Incorporated
The Ghoul of Christmas Past
The Sandman
Jailhouse Golem
Shadow in the Mine
Ghost Writer

Felicity Philips Investigates
To Love and to Perish
Tying the Noose
Aisle Kill Him
A Dress to Die For
Wedding Ceremony Woes

Patricia Fisher Cruise Mysteries
The Missing Sapphire of Zangrabar
The Kidnapped Bride
The Director's Cut
The Couple in Cabin 2124
Doctor Death
Murder on the Dancefloor
Mission for the Maharaja
A Sleuth and her Dachshund in Athens
The Maltese Parrot
No Place Like Home

Patricia Fisher Mystery Adventures
What Sam Knew
Solstice Goat
Recipe for Murder
A Banshee and a Bookshop
Diamonds, Dinner Jackets, and Death
Frozen Vengeance
Mug Shot
The Godmother
Murder is an Artform
Wonderful Weddings and Deadly
Divorces
Dangerous Creatures

Patricia Fisher: Ship's Detective Series
The Ship's Detective
Fitness Can Kill
Death by Pirates
First Dig Two Graves

Albert Smith Culinary Capers
Pork Pie Pandemonium
Bakewell Tart Bludgeoning
Stilton Slaughter
Bedfordshire Clanger Calamity
Death of a Yorkshire Pudding
Cumberland Sausage Shocker
Arbroath Smokie Slaying
Dundee Cake Dispatch
Lancashire Hotpot Peril
Blackpool Rock Bloodshed
Kent Coast Oyster Obliteration
Eton Mess Massacre
Cornish Pasty Conspiracy

Realm of False Gods
Untethered magic
Unleashed Magic
Early Shift
Damaged but Powerful
Demon Bound
Familiar Territory
The Armour of God
Live and Die by Magic
Terrible Secrets

Printed in Great Britain
by Amazon

20124756R00088